INTRODUCING THE TOFF

INTRODUCING THE TOFF

John Creasey

CHIVERS
THORNDIKE

This Large Print book is published by BBC Audiobooks Ltd, Bath, England and by Thorndike Press®, Waterville, Maine, USA.

Published in 2005 in the U.K. by arrangement with Tethered Camel Ltd.

Published in 2005 in the U.S. by arrangement with Tethered Camel Ltd.

U.K. Hardcover   ISBN 1–4056–3439–1 (Chivers Large Print)
U.K. Softcover   ISBN 1–4056–3440–5 (Camden Large Print)
U.S. Softcover   ISBN 0–7862–8150–2 (British Favorites)

The text of this Large Print edition is unabridged.
Other aspects of the book may vary from the original edition.

Set in 16 pt. New Times Roman.

Printed in Great Britain on acid-free paper.

British Library Cataloguing in Publication Data available

Library of Congress Cataloging-in-Publication Data

Creasey, John.
    Introducing the Toff / by John Creasey.
        p.   cm.
    "Thorndike Press large print British favorites."—T.p. verso.
    ISBN 0–7862–8150–2 (lg. print : sc : alk. paper)
    1. Toff (Fictitious character)—Fiction. 2. Private investigators—England—London—Fiction. 3. London—(England)—Fiction.
    4. Large type books. I. Title.
PR6005.R517I58 2005
823'.912—dc22   2005023822

Foreword

RICHARD CREASEY

The Toff—or the Honourable Richard Rollison—was 'born' in the twopenny weekly *Thriller* in 1933 but it was not until 1938 that my father, John Creasey, first published books about him. At once the Toff took on characteristics all his own and became a kind of 'Saint with his feet on the ground.' My father consciously used the Toff to show how well the Mayfair man-about-town could get on with the rough diamonds of the East End.

What gives the Toff his ever-fresh, ever-appealing quality is that he likes people and continues to live a life of glamour and romance while constantly showing (by implication alone) that all men are brothers under the skin.

I am delighted that the Toff is available again to enchant a whole new audience. And proud that my parents named me Richard after such an amazing role-model.

Richard Creasey is Chairman of The Television Trust for the Environment *and, for the last 20 years, has been an executive producer for both BBC and ITV.*

It was John Creasey who introduced him to the

v

world of travel and adventure. Richard and his brother were driven round the world for 465 days in the back of their parents' car when they were five and six years old. In 1992 Richard led 'The Overland Challenge' driving from London to New York via the Bering Strait.

CHAPTER ONE

The Toff Is Curious

In the murky saloon bars of the East End of London and the countless grimy doss-houses in the side streets and alleys branching from the Thames, where the scum of the earth got drunk and the chief topic of conversation was crime, they called the Hon Richard Rollison The Toff. Wherein lie many stories.

At the time of that story with which we are immediately concerned the occupants of those squalid quarters dared not speak the Toff's name without looking furtively over their shoulders, suspicious of any familiar face, fearful that he was among them. He appeared in the most unexpected places and at the most inconvenient times with a twisted grin at the corners of his mouth and his grey eyes glinting, as though he had just communed with the Devil himself and had the Devil's own knowledge of the particular piece of villainy under discussion.

From Lopez the Killer, whose thin-bladed knife had been the foulest weapon in London until the Toff got him, to the lowest-browed pickpocket, they were afraid of the Toff. If he singled out any one of them for attention the victim felt a clammy sensation about his neck,

1

saw a pair of flinty grey eyes wherever he went and was in a state of perpetual ferment, afraid that the Toff was waiting for him at the next corner yet not sure that his lean, powerful figure wasn't behind him, waiting for the right moment to strike.

Nine times out of ten it was easy when the Toff did. He called it psychological terrorism and said unblushingly that he had brought the science to the peak of perfection.

Only a very few among that section of the community conveniently labelled the Underworld denied it. Things came to such a pitch that when the Toff was in the offing it was difficult to hire a cosher—the lowest form of labour in Limehouse and Shadwell—and next-door to impossible to find a man prepared to handle dope or take up a safe drop for blackmail.

The police could be coped with; the ordinary private investigator was a thing of scorn; but the Toff was a thing apart.

Sometimes he worked on his own and sometimes he worked hand-in-glove with the police. Not that he had any great love for the police as such but having one great point in common with them—the suppression of crime, particularly crime with violence or drug-trafficking or blackmail and that vilest trade of all, white slavery—co-operation was sometimes necessary.

On the whole, bad men hated it most when

the Toff worked alone. On those occasions he adopted measures to attain his ends which would certainly have not been approved by the majesty of the law; but they were undoubtedly effective.

The origin of the Toff's campaign against crime was the subject of many wild rumours but in point of fact it was simple. He came down from Cambridge worth half a million of money and with a hatred of dullness. To escape it he travelled the world's farthest corners; and from the dope-dens of Shanghai, the dives of San Francisco and the cess-pools of Marseilles trickled fantastic stories of his speed on the draw, his uncanny accuracy with a knife, the punch like the kick of a mule which he carried in both hands. And always they were concentrated in the one subject— the suppression of crime.

Achmed Dragoli first heard of the Toff from Harry the Pug, a retired prizefighter. Harry's face was completely flattened and his latter years had been spent in the profitable business of pub-keeping and, occasionally, the bumping off of unwanted folk.

The police rarely found the body when Harry the Pug did a job which accounted for Harry's prosperity and the comparative safety of his Shadwell pub, the Red Lion. It said much for the Pug's cunning that so far the Toff had not paid his respects to his particular den.

The two men were sitting in Harry's private

parlour, above the saloon bar. Achmed Dragoli, who had been introduced to the Pug by another gentleman in the trade, made a promising proposition but Harry turned it down flat.

'Not a hope,' he said finally. 'I wouldn't touch it for a thousand thick 'uns. Before we got going we'd have the Toff on the job—and I ain't ready for the rope yet, mister.'

'Mister' was Harry's regular form of address.

Dragoli evinced no signs of disappointment. He was a big man with the curious flowing grace of the East; but his deep-set black eyes with yellowish whites, full lips partly hidden by a silky brown beard, bore silent testimony to that worst of all rogues: the Eastern degenerate.

He spoke good English with a slow, careful enunciation.

'You are frightened of this—Toff?'

Harry the Pug had a thick skin.

'I'll say I am,' he admitted candidly, 'and there ain't a bloke what's come up against him once who wouldn't live through a n'earthquake rather than run into 'im again. I seen the Toff pick up a bigger man than you and pitch 'im over a twelve-foot wall. And I ain't doing no killing this time, Mr. Dragoli. That's final, see?'

'I was told,' said Dragoli cunningly, 'that you had a reputation for doing this work safely.'

Harry patted his large stomach.

'Sure,' he said complacently, 'that's right. Show me the man yer want to git rid of and I'll do it slicker'n any man in town—if it's straightforward. But there's too many loose ends, mister, and'—the Pug's little eyes glinted—'I 'appen to know the Toff's in town. He'd be on our tails in 'arf a shake.' Harry paused and poked his thumbs through the armholes of his gaudy waistcoat. 'Sorry, mister. I know yer money's good. You wouldn't come from where you do if it wasn't. But I ain't takin' no chances with a killing job when the Toff's around.'

Dragoli stood up, shrugging his shoulders. Harry watched him half-way to the door before he spoke again.

'But I don't mind doin' yer a good turn, mister. There's a guy who might take yer, pokin' round town—a Yank. I reckon he ain't met the Toff yet. His name's Garrotty and you'll find him at Blind Sletter's place—the Steam Packet, Lambeth. You know the Steam Packet, don't you?'

Dragoli nodded.

'Yes,' he said in a curiously chanting voice, 'and I've heard of Garrotty. Perhaps it would be as well to give this job to him.'

'He won't turn it down,' said Harry the Pug with assurance. 'He's gittin' tired of doin' nothing. Good night, mister.'

*   *   *

As with many of the Toff's adventures, fate had told him nothing of Achmed Dragoli before the affair near the London-Chelmsford road. But it is fairly safe to assume that he knew nothing beyond the fact that Garrotty, known to be a killer, had slipped past the police and was somewhere in England. The connection between Dragoli and Garrotty was yet unknown and the sinister influence of the Black Circle was barely suspected. Otherwise the Toff would not have been caught napping; that never happened when he was out on "business."

Yet even after the first brush he felt that the murder on the Chelmsford road went deeper even than it appeared.

The Toff was driving across the low-lying Essex countryside beneath a harvest moon shimmering silver from blue-grey heavens, dimmed now and again by little white puffs of cloud. There was an exhilarating nip in the air and he was pleasantly relaxed after a day's country-house cricket at his father's Norfolk home. Only a little affair at the Old Bailey next morning, when he was due to give testimony anent the murderous activities of Lopez the Killer, would have made him do the journey that night instead of waiting till the following day.

He was three miles out of Chelmsford when he first saw the big car; the light of the moon showed him the flying black shape at the top of a rise nearly a mile away. The car carried no headlights.

'It looks,' murmured the Toff, 'like a thorough-going road-hog. The fool must be travelling at seventy. It's a night for optimism but if we're not careful there'll be a smash with a capital S.'

He eased down the engine of his slinky Allard, pushed his finger on the button of the electric horn and kept it there. It blared out a long, continuous warning, urgent and imperative, through the quiet of the night.

The Toff then prepared for the worst, braking to a standstill, levering his lean body from his seat and sizing up the chances of leaping out if the onrushing car didn't slow down. Some men might have got out first and thought about it afterwards. The Toff would stick it to the last minute. At a pinch he could jump clear of the bracken edge alongside the road.

In spite of the screeching of the Toff's horn, the car still came on; and, as it came nearer, its speed became more apparent. The little yellow orbs of its wing lamps were visible now, twisting and turning with the narrow road. Gradually the hum of its engine impinged itself on the Toff's ears.

'Not so good,' he murmured and sent out a

series of long blasts on the electric horn.

The car—a Daimler he saw now—swung into the Toff's straight stretch; only a hundred yards separated the two automobiles. Those little yellow orbs glowed weirdly in the pale light; the Daimler looked unreal, a ghostly monster of speed, ninety yards away—eighty-seventy.

'The fool must be blind or deaf,' growled the Toff. 'And I'd like to know why he's cutting that speed.'

But the time for speculation had gone; it was a matter of seconds now. The Toff pressed his horn again and flexed the muscles of his calves. He saw the big car looming towards him, heard the great engine roaring, saw the little yellow orbs rushing at his eyes.

Then suddenly he relaxed and slid back in his seat, the corners of his mouth turning down.

The driver of the Daimler—a vague silhouette of head and shoulders to the Toff—leaned forward and clutched at his brake. The night air howled with the screech as the big car slithered to a standstill.

'An end to that spot of bother,' thought the Toff.

But for once in his life he was taken in, simply because he was not expecting trouble. As he groped for his clutch, intending to ease forward a yard or two and get within complaining distance of the driver, he was plunged suddenly into a blinding sea of light. The Daimler's headlights were switched full on.

The Toff darted his hands towards his eyes. It was the last thing he had expected and the surprise, if it was intended for such, was completely successful. Momentarily he forgot himself and said things across the dazzle to the driver of the Daimler that would have made a Bowery tough turn pink.

But as quickly as it flared his anger evaporated; and as he cooled down he heard the soft purr of the Daimler's engine. The big car was being eased forward through that ocean of blinding light.

The Toff felt strangely still. He sat motionless for a second but for the widening of his eyes as the headlights dimmed and then went out.

The moon prevented pitch darkness from coming and the Toff looked about him very intently. It was queer; and queer things were the Toff's stock-in-trade.

The radiator of the Daimler was only a yard away. The driver was leaning out of the window and the first impression that the Toff had of him was of yellowish eyes glowing in the moonlight. Then Rollison saw the smooth dark beard, the rounded regular features; and he knew that he was looking at a gentleman from the East.

At that moment Rollison was more

concerned with the man's road-hogging than his appearance yet for the Toff his protest was strangely mild.

'You weren't asking for trouble, were you? What would have happened if I hadn't been looking?'

His sarcasm was lost on the foreigner. The man's head came forward; on closer inspection the Toff saw the crow's-feet gathered in the corners of his queer eyes and the furrows across his brow beneath the black Homburg hat thrust too far back on his head.

'I must ask you to excuse me, sir.' The voice was smooth, uncannily suggesting the swaying incantation of the East, though the English was word perfect. 'I am in a very great hurry. Perhaps you will be good enough to reverse to a wider stretch of road?'

Rollison was suddenly conscious of unreasoning antagonism. On top of the shilly-shallying with the headlights, the man's manner annoyed him. He could have forgiven the haste but not the attitude.

Perhaps because of that sudden feeling of hostility his voice was unusually mild.

'I'm in a hurry too,' he drawled. 'You do the honours,' and he smiled provokingly.

The baleful eyes narrowed. The Toff almost felt the other's effort to restrain a tirade of abuse but he admitted that it was kept well in check.

'I hope you will not insist, sir,' said the

10

driver. 'Perhaps if I explain that I am a doctor you will better understand my fast driving. This is my third important case tonight. And it is extremely urgent.'

Was it? wondered the Toff.

The tired eyes, and the look of near-exhaustion, bore some testimony to the man's words. It was a reasonable explanation but it didn't ring true. It made the Toff very thoughtful and turned him very polite.

On the face of it there was only one thing to do, for the Toff disliked the thought of denying aid to the weak and ailing and said as much as he slipped the sports car into reverse. There was a wider patch of road a hundred yards or so back.

The little car slid backwards. The doctor let in his clutch and the Daimler crawled forward, still no more than two yards away from the smaller car's radiator. Whatever else, the man was certainly in a hurry—and, thought Rollison, something was playing old Harry with his nerves. The twitching eyes and nostrils told of a state of high tension. It occurred to the Toff that anyone doctored by him at the moment would be in Queer Street.

But there were other things occupying the Toff's attention. As he moved backwards, without hurrying, suspicion was taking a more definite shape in his mind. A little imp of doubt grew restive and one problem loomed larger than the rest.

Why had the self-styled doctor switched on the headlights?

Rollison, staring hard, centred his gaze on the grey curtains of the saloon immediately behind the driver. They gaped a trifle where they overlapped; suddenly the Toff's lips tightened and the little imp of doubt grinned widely.

If everything were straight and above-board, the doctor would hardly be carrying a passenger in the rear when the seat next to him was vacant. Yet the red glow of a cigarette spread for a second and then died down.

Someone was in the back of the Daimler.

'Stranger and stranger,' murmured the Toff; he was beginning to enjoy himself.

As the two cars crawled in ghostly succession, he formed an opinion in the manner that had made him the best-hated man in the shadier purlieus of the East End.

After the driver of the Daimler had jammed on his brakes and slithered to safety he had deliberately dazzled the Toff by switching on the headlights. Obviously that had been to give that mysterious passenger time to draw the curtains and hide his face. And the passenger was not overloaded with little grey cells, otherwise he would have doused the cigarette.

The Toff's conjecture was not water-tight but it was sound enough to rouse that curiosity. He had positive doubts of the doctor's story but didn't voice them. There might be more in this than met the eye but it would not be revealed by putting awkward questions. Nor, unless things happened quickly, would it be revealed that night.

The cars, still nose to nose, reached the wider stretch of road. The Toff swung his Allard close to the hedge; brambles scratched along the wings as he smiled at the man with the beard. A more affable, anger-appeased motorist would have been hard to find.

'Here we are,' the Toff said. 'Go steady for the next half-mile. The road twists about a lot and everybody doesn't know it as well as I do.' The 'doctor' ignored the thrust.

'You have my very best thanks, sir. I very much appreciate your courtesy.'

'Delighted,' lied the Toff and waved his hand.

His fingers could have brushed the body of the Daimler as it squeezed past. Taking a cigarette from his case, he struck a match as the doctor, in line with him, nodded with that touch of condescending arrogance which had annoyed Rollison before and angered him again now.

He bit back an acid comment, made an ineffectual effort to see through the drawn curtains, then shrugged his shoulders. It was a promising little mystery nipped in the bud. A pity.

Then his jaw hardened and subconsciously his hand moved towards his fob pocket where, in days of "off" business, he parked his gun. For out of the corners of his eyes he saw the curtains widen; the mysterious passenger was curious.

The Toff was very wary, even before he saw the gun poking towards him from the rear window.

CHAPTER TWO

And Makes A Discovery

The Toff's teeth snapped and he ducked, grabbing for his own gun. But before he could draw, the air behind him was punctured by two yellow flashes of flame. Two soft "zutts" told of an efficient silencer; lead-nosed bullets banged into the rear of the sports car.

The Toff screwed round to take aim, still keeping under cover of his car's hood. Before his finger touched the trigger the air was split again by two yellow flashes; a bullet tore into the rear offside wheel and the little car lurched on one side as the tyre burst with a deafening report.

The Toff felt the machine quiver from bonnet to tail-lamp; he stumbled forward, losing his grip on his gun and banging his nose painfully on the dashboard. Tears swam in his eyes, half-blinding him as he crouched out of the line of fire. He was burning to take a shot at the gunman but he knew better than to show so much as the tip of his nose. He had been caught for a sucker; there was no need to act like one.

He made a lightning review of the possibilities as he regained his automatic. Was the attack a deliberate and planned attempt on his life? It would not have been the first; a hundred rogues hated him enough for it. Or had Providence rocketed him into trouble for its own sweet sake?

When the danger was past he could reason it out. Meanwhile, would the gunman in the Daimler take another blinder or

The sudden, fierce whirr of the Daimler's engine answered him. The big car began to move and the black roof, all that Rollison permitted himself to see, slid along the hedges.

'They're off,' he muttered and his fingers tightened round the handle of his gun. A thought was scurrying through his mind, tempting, enticing. If he stood up from his cover and emptied his gun after the Daimler there was a sound chance of sending the big car into the hedge; what happened after that would be in the hands of the gods.

It was a beautiful thought. The Toff licked his lips over it and his eyes sparkled. Nine times out of ten he would have taken a chance and been confident of getting away with it. But this time . . .

15

Reason told him that there was something back along the road from which the Daimler was flying and which the gunman was very anxious to keep undiscovered for a while. It would be better to let the Daimler go, to hurry back along the road and find out what there was to find. For once he played for safety.

Still crouching, he saw that flying roof twist with a bend in the road out of shooting range. The Daimler was a hundred yards away, still gathering speed, weird and ghostly beneath the moon. Watching it, Rollison felt a queer intuition that he was only on the fringe of trouble; and a question persisted in his mind.

What would he find?

One thing now seemed certain. The attack had much more behind it than the attempted annihilation of the Hon Richard Rollison. Otherwise the shooting would have had a more personal note from the outset.

With which comforting thought the Toff stepped into the road and surveyed the damage. A wing of his car was badly dented and a piece was chipped from the number-plate; but that, apart from the punctured tyre, was the extent of the trouble.

'It might have been a lot worse,' he consoled himself, dipping into the tool-box for the jack. He had a habit, when alone, of talking aloud, usually in the plural. It fortified him.

He started to take the wheel off. 'We ought to have the spare wheel on inside ten minutes,' he told the world at large, 'and then we shall see what they wanted to stop us from seeing. And it looks as if we shall be busy in the not too distant future.'

And again, as he spoke, his eyes were like flints and his lips were pressed together in a thin line. Many things were passing through his mind but he told the world nothing about them.

A fraction over the ten minutes later, Rollison straightened his back and sighed. He tossed the tools back in the box, flung the busted wheel into the rear seat and swung himself into the driving position.

The engine hummed to a touch on the switch. He let in his clutch gently and turned round. As the car went back he looked right and left on the shimmering surface of the road. He did not propose to miss a thing.

A quarter of a mile dropped behind and the gentle hum of his engine harmonised again with the quiet of the night. The moon was so bright that he switched off the headlights; the ribbon of road unwinding in front of him seemed as empty of trouble as the blue-grey sky.

And then, taking a bend slowly, Rollison caught his first glimpse of the night's secret.

Black and grim at the side of the road were the shattered remains of a big car.

The Toff stared for a moment then tightened his grip round the steering-wheel.

'I had a feeling,' he reminded himself softly, 'that there was trouble and I fancy I was right.'

He drew close to the wreckage. Nothing else moved; no sound came. The hush of the night seemed to whisper death—death which was hiding amidst the ruins of that smashed-up car.

As Rollison pulled in beside the wrecked car he saw that it was a saloon Packard with its radiator buried in the ditch at the side of the road where it had plunged helplessly. The body was crushed and twisted, the wings ripped away and the windscreen was smashed into a thousand pieces.

Rollison stepped out of his car looking more for what had caused the smash than the effect of it. But for the Daimler and the attack which had been made on him he would have jumped to the conclusion that it had been due to the driver's recklessness. Now no such possibility entered his mind. The Packard had been deliberately wrecked by the man with the beard and his sharp-shooting passenger—and the Toff's car had been put out of action to give the attackers a clear get-away before the alarm could be raised.

The Toff squeezed through the narrow gap between the car and the hedge. Thorns caught his coat and scratched his fingers but he hardly noticed them. For he caught his first glimpse of the victim of the smash—the body of the man slumped in the driving-seat amidst the wreckage. And as he saw him the Toff knew that there was not a chance in a thousand of the man being alive.

The victim's right leg was doubled back beneath him. His eyes were glazed and sightless. One arm was bent across his chest with his hand near his chin, as though he had darted his hand upwards to ward off the sudden terror that had loomed in front of him.

The moon shimmered on blood coming from a hole in the forehead and there was no mistaking the cause of that wound. It was a bullet-hole.

Rollison's shoe tapped the surface of the road. In his mind's eye there sprang a picture of a bearded face and a pair of yellowish eyes.

Then he found himself thinking, unreasonably, inconsequently, of a name.

'Garrotty's in England,' he muttered. 'Garrotty the Yank. And this is gunman's work.'

He jerked himself together and bent down, feeling for the man's pulse. It was a mere formality; there was no movement, and he had expected none. But he felt something damp against his hand, some-thing which shone red in the moonlight. The man had been shot through the chest as well as the head.

Rollison stayed where he was for a moment. The face of the man was arresting, even in death. Saturnine, swarthy, like that of a man who had lived for many years in hot climates, there was a sardonic twist to those still lips, as though the man had died with mockery in his eyes.

Rollison took his hand away, stood up and peered about him. There would be the devil to pay for this brutal murder on the country road. Without doubt, it had traces of gangster work; in the vernacular, the man had been put on the spot and the killers had made a good job of it.

Then Rollison, who was not easily surprised, saw something which made his heart miss a beat.

Odds and ends of steel were strewn about the road, mixed with a few pitiful possessions of the victim. A watch dangled from its chain which had got caught in the running board, the glass smashed but the mechanism was still ticking. A case, half-full of broken cigarettes, was close to it; and close by a trilby hat rested on its crown.

Then, entirely out of keeping with the rest and some distance from the wrecked car, was a woman's shoe.

Rollison picked it up. It drew his mind from the horror of the murder.

'Puzzle,' he muttered, 'find the lady.'

The shoe was a small, satin-covered creation, more suited for a ballroom than a journey by road. There was a film of dust over the satin and here and there it was scratched and torn. Half-way up the heel was a patch of mud—and it was the mud which made the Toff frown. For it was wet.

In five minutes the Toff had learned enough to make the owner of the shoe a central figure in the mystery. In the ditch alongside the road ran a sluggish stream of water, more mud than anything else. And there were deeply set footprints, fitting the shoe to a T at one place and blurred out of recognition in another while on the thorns of the hedge were a wisp or two of finely woven cloth.

It was easy to reconstruct the scene. The girl had been travelling in the wrecked car, he reckoned, and had managed to get out of it before the smash. But her bid for safety had failed; almost certainly she had been in the Daimler, hidden from sight by those drawn curtains. No wonder he had been blinded to make sure that he saw nothing inside.

His eyes were very hard as he turned away, stuffing the shoe into his coat pocket, and slipped into the car. The quicker the police knew of the hold-up the better but it was possible that the shoe would help him, the Toff, to find a short cut to the murderers and he looked on the shoe as his own special clue.

CHAPTER THREE

The Pug Is Visited

Rollison might not have had the true citizen's regard for the police but he treated that fine body of men with a measure of respect which they rarely appreciated. For instance, he spoke over the telephone from an AA box half a mile from the wrecked Packard to one Chief Inspector McNab, of Scotland Yard, who was no bosom friend. He told McNab just where a man had been killed near the London-Chelmsford road and he promised McNab he would make sure that no one interfered with the wreckage until the police arrived.

'Yes,' he said, 'it was certainly murder—gun-play, Mac.'

It took McNab, a burly, square jawed Scot, exactly forty-four minutes to reach the scene of the crime, accompanied by three equally grim-visaged local men. McNab found the Packard and the murdered man just as he had been told. But he did not see the Toff, although the Toff saw him. It was the kind of thing that savoured of black magic but in point of fact it was easy.

The Toff simply ran his car to a convenient lane off the main road after telephoning the police and then perched himself on a five-barred gate near the Packard, smoking many cigarettes and persuading occasional motorists that he had had a smash and that they would have to go back for a bit, making a long detour, unless they cared to wait for the breakdown gang. None of them waited.

Thanks to the moon, he saw the police car coming. McNab, whom he knew well, was easily recognisable. Then the Toff slipped off the gate, hurried across the field to his bus and started for London.

He did not expect things to happen quickly and was quite prepared to await developments. Yet the affair became suddenly even more significant because of the hush-hush attitude taken by the police.

For when the Toff read the morning paper over the breakfast table the murder had no front-page headlines, although it undoubtedly deserved them from a journalistic point of view. When he found the report there was nothing to suggest that there had been anything more unusual than a road smash. No mention was made at all of the gun-shot wounds in the man's forehead and the chest.

'Funnier and funnier,' thought the Toff and then read the only useful piece of news in the paragraph. The dead man's name was Goldman—Paul Goldman—and he had recently returned to England after a long sojourn in Turkey.

'I could have guessed most of that myself,'

murmured the Toff as he got up from the table. 'I wonder what McNab will have to say about it?'

McNab telephoned him early and asked him to go round to the Yard after he had given evidence against Lopez the Killer. When the Toff arrived he found the Chief Inspector almost fussy, which was merely a device to persuade the Toff not to put up difficulties over the hush-hush business, and the Toff was not surprised.

Nor was he surprised when McNab refused to talk much. He agreed, generously, that there were a thousand Daimlers which might have answered his description of the murder car. Nor could the police be expected to put their hands on the driver of the Daimler because he had a beard and looked like an Egyptian.

But there was not a shred of doubt that the police knew more about the affair than they professed and that gave the Toff to think, furiously.

He did not say so.

'So we're stuck,' he suggested to McNab. They were in the latter's poky office at Scotland Yard which possessed only one comfortable chair— McNab's—and he showed no inclination to linger.

The Scot grunted.

'Maybe. We know Garrotty's about, mind ye.'

'Och, aye,' grinned Rollison, 'and we might guess that Garrotty killed Goldman. But we don't know anything about the man with the beard'—the Toff's grin widened—'and we don't know much about Goldman himself. Or do we?' He arched his brows. 'Seeing that I found him, it doesn't seem fair to leave me out in the cold.'

McNab rubbed his chin and then grew talkative, which told the Toff that the Scot was giving nothing away beyond a little information which might be picked up from the later editions of the Press.

'Goldman,' said McNab portentously but with feeling, 'was a damn' fool. He meddled with things that were too big for him—'

The Toff interrupted.

'A point for you,' he conceded. 'Goldman meddled—I'm meddling. Sounds like a conjugation of verbs, doesn't it, Mac?' He beamed and waved his hand airily. 'But don't let me stop you.'

McNab bit the end off a cigar.

'You're getting funny,' he growled. 'See here, Rolleeson. The man Goldman was bad from beginning to end. He knew the inside of Pentonville before he went abroad and then mixed himself up with a gang of thieves. You know the result.'

'Death, via the said crooks?'

'Never you mind,' growled McNab. 'I'm thinking that this is a big thing, Rolleeson.

Ye'd better be careful.'

'Of Garrotty?' demanded the Toff.

McNab scowled.

'I'm not thinking of Garrotty.'

Then the Toff took a shot in the dark with two reasons behind it. He was anxious to learn all he could and he tried to bluff McNab into speaking more plainly. And, more important, he was worried about the girl. If McNab didn't know about her, the Toff realised he was withholding information of much gravity by not speaking and that information might prove invaluable to the girl, might even save her life.

'I know you're not,' he went on and his eyes narrowed. 'I wonder if you're thinking of the girl in the case?'

McNab's lips tightened.

'So you know about her, do you?'

'I do,' said the Toff and felt easier in his mind.

The policeman lit his small cigar slowly.

'Well,' he said at last, 'maybe you can tell us where she is, Rolleeson?'

The Toff shook his head.

'Then,' said McNab, 'all I'm saying is—be careful—verra careful!'

'I will,' promised the Toff and smiled widely and took his leave of the Inspector.

Jolly, the Toff's personal servant, major-domo, chef, valet, counsellor and bodyguard, grew apprehensively aware that his employer was brooding over something important. Jolly, a lugubrious soul, knew nothing of the satin shoe which was hidden in the Toff's Gresham Terrace flat. But he saw the added gaiety in the Toff's manner and knew that the Toff deserted the flat more frequently than usual. Further, the Toff warned him to keep the door closed on all pipe-fitters from the Gas Company, gentlemen from the Electric Light Corporation and representatives of the Metropolitan Water Board. The Toff did not believe in taking unnecessary chances; he even went so far as to have his food specially prepared and, in effect, hygienically sealed. Safety was much better than poisoned soup.

The three days immediately following the murder were not entirely without incident, however, although the Toff admitted that he started the ball rolling.

On the morning of the second day the Toff, resplendent in faultless grey and driving a Rolls-Bentley, which was a car of cars indeed, went to Limehouse and Shadwell. He knew, as he turned in and out of the cobbled streets, that the car was recognised and that word was spreading that he was about. A thought tickled his vanity: a dozen gentlemen were shaking in their shoes.

But the one man in all Shadwell who felt that he was safe from the Toff's attentions had a shock.

He was sitting in his parlour above the saloon bar, looking out of the window and seeing, but not noticing, the masts of many Dutch trawlers docked alongside the Thames and the smokeless, but grimy, funnels of a few idle steamers. He knew nothing of the Rolls-Bentley which drew up in front of the Red Lion—the parlour was at the back—until Squinty burst into the room in a pretty state of funk.

'What the 'ell's the matter with you?' snarled Harry the Pug who had been dreaming rosy dreams. Then he saw the card trembling in Squinty's knuckly hand.

He felt a lump rise suddenly from his stomach to his throat. His voice was cracked.

'The Toff!'

Squinty didn't say a word. He was still seeing the incredibly thin and immaculate man whose grey eyes had seemed to burn into his soul—which was nearly impossible for Squinty was more brute than man.

Harry the Pug felt very cold. He recognised the little picture on one side of the card and did not trouble to read the other, introducing the Hon Richard Rollison of Gresham Terrace, W1. The picture was simple. Just a top hat set at a rakish angle and beneath it a monocle, cigarette in jaunty holder and bow tie. The Toff called it his trade mark and used it only on business.

The Pug found his voice again but he was still pale.

'You ruddy fool! What did you bring it in

28

for? Tell him I'm out. Tell him anything! I won't see him.' His voice rose to a squeak. 'Don't you understand that, you squint-eyed fool? I won't see him—'

Then he looked past Squinty and his mouth stuck open.

'Perfectly understood,' murmured the Toff from the door. 'Too bad I followed Squinty up, wasn't it?'

He walked softly across the parlour, reached Squinty and snapped his fingers close to a cauliflower ear. Squinty vanished and the Toff watched him close the door.

Then he turned to Harry the Pug.

'Now we're alone,' he drawled and sat down without being asked. 'Keeping busy, Harry?'

The Pug bit his lip. This was the meeting he had tried more than anything else in the world to prevent. Now it had happened out of the blue. The Toff was sitting elegantly in front of him, lean hands playing idly with his cane, flinty eyes staring—staring.

Harry the Pug felt dreadfully afraid but no one had ever called him yellow. His thick lips split.

'What are you after, mister?'

'If it eases your mind,' said the Toff blandly, 'I'm not after you—yet. Information, Harry, with a capital "I". Do we have a spot before you talk?'

Harry ignored the hint and licked his lips.

'I don't know a thing,' he said.

'Too bad,' murmured the Toff. 'I had it from very good authority that you know where Garrotty the Yank is staying at the moment. Much too bad!'

'Never heard of him,' lied Harry who hated the drawling mockery of that 'too bad.' 'See here, guv'nor, I'm on the level. I don't say I ain't been a bit gay in my time but I'm finished now and . . .'

He trailed off for the Toff's eyes narrowed.

'Stow it,' he said sharply. 'Where's Garrotty?'

Under that frosty stare Harry the Pug wilted, as many a better man would have done. He shifted his chair back and the legs squeaked across the linoleum. The knobbly hand which he pushed over his flat brow was unsteady.

Garrotty was nothing to him, anyhow.

'Last I heard of him,' he muttered, 'he was at the Steam Packet, Lambeth. But I ain't working with him, mister, s'welp me, I ain't!'

'If it eases your mind,' repeated the Toff smoothly, 'I know you ain't.' His voice hardened. 'But you had the chance, didn't you?'

Harry kept silent. The thought that the Toff might know of his meeting with Dragoli made his stomach turn. Because the Toff, with his uncanny knack of squeezing information from the dregs of the underworld, was just as likely to know of some of the darker deeds in

Harry's past—not to mention his present.

The Toff broke the silence.

'I'll take yes for an answer, my little man.'

He stood up, so quickly that Harry didn't notice he had moved until he stood by the window, leaning against the framework and staring across the parlour. His voice was smooth.

If the police knew half what I know about you, Harry, you wouldn't be away from the rope for more than a couple of months. But you haven't been working for a long time now—and I might let you off . . .'

Harry turned in his chair, his nostrils distended and the blood showing red beneath the several scars on his flattened face. He knew that the Toff was playing with him cat-and-mouse, as if delighting in the mental torture. But it went deeper than that. It says much for Harry's fear of the Toff that he did not once think of using his knife.

What did the Toff want?

'I'll tell you,' drawled Rollison with whom mind-reading of a certain nature was an art. His voice dropped. 'Achmed Dragoli's been here. What was he after?'

The Pug felt horribly afraid.

'Who—who's Dragoli?'

'He's the Egyptian gentleman,' said the Toff patiently, 'who came to see you a few days ago with a proposition. After seeing you he got in touch with Garrotty the Yank. What was he after?'

Harry the Pug squirmed. He was in a hell of a fix and he knew it. The trouble was knowing just how much the Toff was bluffing and how much he really knew.

But there was one thing about the Toff which was generally admitted. He never went back on his word. If he promised to let Harry alone—

The Toff moved suddenly to the table where Harry was sitting. He stared down at the ex-bruiser and there was a wicked smile at the corners of his lips.

'I know what you're thinking,' he claimed gently. 'Listen, Harry. Spill everything, don't add any lies, and I'll leave you alone for your past. That doesn't cover anything you do in the future.'

Harry's little eyes shifted first, then his lips opened.

'To start you off,' drawled the Toff, who saw that his victory was won so far and decided the time for his bluff had come, 'he mentioned a man named Goldman. I know Garrotty killed Goldman and I want to know why. See?'

Harry saw. And he was afraid because what little he knew might not satisfy the Toff.

'He didn't say who,' he muttered. 'Believe it or not, mister, he didn't mention a name. All he said was there was a yob he wanted out of the way and somehow he got an idea I'd do it.' The Pug grew very indignant. 'And I turned him flat, mister, you kin take it from me! I never mixed meself up in a game like that, an' I ain't goin' ter—'

'Of course you isn't,' drawled the Toff. 'But he told you something else, Harry. What?'

Harry the Pug looked like an ape in a tight corner. The blood showed livid in his many scars.

'He didn't, mister, s'welp me! He just said he'd got a job and it had to be finished quick.'

The Toff's eyes sparkled for that was worth knowing. But he wanted more and he had an idea that Harry could give it to him. His lips were very close together.

'Don't call me mister,' he said unpleasantly. 'And don't try to fool me, Harry.' He paused for a second, leaned towards the Pug and then he drawled:

'Who sent Dragoli to you?'

It happened as he had expected it to happen.

The Pug's face literally blanched. In those piggish eyes leapt an expression of fear which the Toff knew was not inspired by himself.

Harry's lips worked convulsively.

'What—what do you mean?'

'Stop playing dumb,' the Toff urged. 'Someone sent Dragoli to you—and you know who it was.'

For a full minute the Toff thought that the sinister influence which had a stranglehold on Harry the Pug would frustrate him. But suddenly the Pug's resistance drooped.

'Supposin' I tell you? You don't know 'em, anyway.'

'I know lots of things,' said the Toff lightly, 'that you wouldn't dream. Stop stalling, Harry.'

The Pug's voice was hoarse. His eyes went to and fro, furtive, fearful.

'If you will have it, mister—it was the Black Circle.'

For a moment there was dead silence in the room. The Toff stared at the Pug and the Pug drew back. For the Toff's eyes were like steel, making the Pug squirm.

And yet the Toff was just thinking blindly. The Black Circle meant nothing at all to him; he had never heard of it. But it was a big thing in Harry the Pug's sinful life.

The Toff tried another shot.

'The Black Circle, is it?' he said. 'Well, what does that association do for its living, Harry?'

The Pug kept quiet for a moment. His little eyes were darting to and fro, fearfully.

'I daren't tell you,' he said at last. 'I just daren't, mister!'

The Toff knew then that he had come up against a brick wall. It made him very thoughtful for if the Black Circle was dangerous enough to make Harry the Pug refuse to squeal, it was very big indeed.

Yet he did not want to force the Pug's hand too far. Up to now Harry had been useful; he still would be if handled properly.

'And so,' said the Toff smoothly, 'you won't come across.'

'I daren't, I tell you! They'd kill me if I squealed.'

'That wouldn't do any harm,' the Toff said unkindly. Then he grinned and took a chance shot. 'So they'd kill you, would they—just as they killed Goldman. And'—he stared very hard into the Pug's shifty eyes—'for the same reason, Harry?'

The Pug hesitated.

'Talk, friend, or any promise to you won't count.'

'Well,' muttered Harry reluctantly, 'I think Goldman was going to squeal on the Circle, mister—'

'Fine!' breathed the Toff.

The Pug's admission meant a lot. Goldman had been killed because he was ready to betray Dragoli and the mysterious Black Circle. That helped. He was as much in the dark as ever about the girl who had been with Goldman when he had been murdered.

Again a silence fell over the room, tense, expectant. The Pug stared fearfully at his interrogator.

'Fine!' repeated the Toff suddenly and made another thrust, although he doubted whether Harry could help him much. 'Where does the girl come in?'

The Pug was surprised into gaping silence. He did not even protest that he knew nothing.

'All right,' said the Toff ironically. 'I'll believe you.'

Then it seemed to the Pug that the Toff disappeared. One moment he was in the room and the next he was gone. The Toff had that uncanny knack of being somewhere else before a man realised that he had moved at all.

For the moment the Toff had learned all there was to learn from Harry the Pug and he had learned a great deal more than he had expected. He knew now why Goldman had been killed and it was easy to agree with McNab that the dead man was crooked through and through.

He knew that Dragoli was an agent of the Black Circle and if he was completely fogged by the game that the organisation was playing he did not intend to be in the dark much longer.

There were other things. Why had the police held back the news of the murder? And—more important—where did the Lady of the Shoe come in?

The Toff didn't know but he had an ingenious mind. He wondered if the girl had known any or all of what Goldman had sold his life for. If she did, it was a black outlook for her.

'But not so black,' said the Toff suddenly, as he swung the Rolls-Bentley into the Mile End Road, 'as it would have been if I hadn't learned that Garrotty is staying at the Steam

Packet, Lambeth. Dragoli won't be far away, I'll wager.'

As had happened before, he would have won his bet.

As befitted the occasion, he was very thoughtful on the drive to his flat. So thoughtful that when he reached Gresham Terrace and found a carefully packed parcel, shaped like a hat-box and labelled with the sacred name of a certain famous hatter, he took it to the bathroom and turned the hot water on, soaking the package for an hour before opening it.

Undoubtedly he bought his hats from that firm. But when he cut the string and found the soddened body of a blood-lusting tarantula whose first bite would have sent him to a very unpleasant death, he was glad that he had been careful.

It was very quick work indeed. He must have been shadowed from Harry the Pug's and his trailers must have taken it for granted that Harry would squeal something, which was bad for Harry. But the Toff, who was very thorough, had more than an idea that the Black Circle was ruthless in the extreme and he had been on the look-out for attacks.

The nature of it annoyed him. It was high time he had an interview with Dragoli, the mystery man from the Middle East.

CHAPTER FOUR

The Steam Packet

On the day that the Toff called on Harry the Pug, the second waiter at the Steam Packet, which is at the corner of Duke Street and York Road, Lambeth with a fine view of the Houses of Parliament from the top windows, wrote a maudlin letter of apology to Blind Sletter who owned the Steam Packet. He had, it appeared, met with an accident and he would not be able to work for some weeks to come.

Blind Sletter did not read the note because he could not; his interest was negligible, however, when Castillo, his manager, told him about it.

'Get another man,' said Sletter plaintively. He was a very old, white-haired gentleman, held in high esteem by those who didn't know him well enough. Such a harmless, well-meaning old soul. 'You can wait on the private rooms, Castillo,' he finished up.

Castillo, a Spaniard of uncertain lineage, bowed from force of habit and went out to look after the running of the restaurant, including the hiring of a new waiter.

The Steam Packet was one of those semi-high-class restaurants with which London abounds. Just too far from things theatrical to lure the West End crowds, it had a large clientele from goggle-eyed suburbanites who were easily persuaded to believe that it was the real thing.

A contributory factor to its success was its absolute respectability beneath its shroud of daring, or scantily-clad, ballet dancers. No one, least of all the police who are chronically suspicious of restaurants, suspected the many strange things which changed hands over Blind Sletter's plain desk in his simple office at the extreme end of the Steam Packet's premises.

Sletter passed dope and jewels and bonds, if they were safe enough, and he had a rich picking.

Also—with which the Toff was concerned— he had a number of private rooms of which the local authorities were not aware. They were built immediately beneath the main restaurant but they were approached only by a subterranean passage from a house nearly a quarter of a mile away or by Sletter's secret entrance. Only Sletter, Castillo and the injured waiter knew of the second means of access, apart from certain privileged guests.

As Harry the Pug had learned, by that mysterious telepathy which is the copyright of the underworld, Garrotty the Yank was enjoying the hospitality of Blind Sletter.

Garrotty was just a gangster without any frills. America had grown too hot for him and he had managed to slide into England, taking refuge at Sletter's because he could afford to pay big money for his security. But Garrotty, essentially a man of action, had grown tired of mooning around and when Dragoli had made his offer he had been very pleased to accept.

Sletter raised no objections to the presence of the crook. If he had heard of Goldman's murder he did not say so. In any case, he had heard of the Black Circle and he was a wise man, knowing what he could tackle and what was best left alone.

There was another visitor who was called a guest and of her Blind Sletter was not so happy in his mind.

He had been in the same room as the girl on several occasions and he knew that she was young and that her voice was pleasant. He knew, too, that she was afraid of Garrotty and that her presence at the Steam Packet was not voluntary. But Garrotty and Dragoli assured the blind man that there was no danger of the girl being traced to the so respectable sanctuary; and, perforce, Sletter let her stay.

If she had put Sletter's reckoning out, she had done the same for the two crooks. Dragoli was in two minds about her for she had been with Goldman on the night of the murder and for some days before. Dragoli kept her alive because he believed that she knew the secret which Goldman had taken with him to the grave.

Dragoli had to learn that secret. Sometimes

Goldman's voice taunted him, even now, for Goldman had died bravely with mockery on his lips.

'You can kill me, Dragoli. You will, anyhow. But you're on the spot yourself and they'll get you.'

Dragoli had stared wickedly into those mocking eyes. Goldman had talked just for the sake of talking.

Ten yards away Garrotty had been chasing after the girl who had made a sudden dash for freedom. The moon had shimmered down on the grim drama.

Then Dragoli said thinly, 'What you know dies with you, Goldman.'

Goldman had died—but before his passing, with a twisted grin at his lips, he had mocked:

'Dies with me, does it? Don't you—believe it—Dragoli. It's on paper! In—black and—white!'

Then Goldman had coughed—a dreadful, racking cough. Dragoli's gun barked again; Goldman's forehead took the bullet dead in the middle. But the seed of doubt was planted in the Egyptian's mind.

Goldman had put his knowledge on paper— knowledge which could betray the vital secrets of the Black Circle.

Because of which the girl lived.

*   *   *

41

The new waiter at the Steam Packet was a very tall, lean man with a vacant expression, a hang-dog air and a professed anxiety concerning the welfare of his wife and children. Castillo, who knew that the surest way to make a man hold his tongue and close his eyes when necessary was to endanger domestic ties of this nature, overlooked certain difficulties of references and engaged the man.

For three nights the waiter proved a model. So much so that Castillo allowed him to take over part of his duties which he did without complaint. On the fourth day those duties were so onerous that the waiter found it necessary to present himself at the Steam Packet shortly after two o'clock instead of five. None of the kitchen staff objected and it so happened that Sletter had gone out on one of his rare but lengthy journeys into the West End and Castillo had taken the opportunity to indulge in frivolous entertainment in his own room.

Just after three o'clock the new man disappeared from the kitchen; no one saw him go. Nor did they see him move along the passages to Sletter's private room, nor see him fiddle with the lock, unfasten it with a skeleton key and slip inside.

Once in the room there was a remarkable transformation in the appearance of the waiter. His obsequious air disappeared. His lean body straightened and his grey eyes were very hard. Apart from his loose-fitting waiter's clothes, he looked who he was—the Toff.

He knew that he had to work quickly for Sletter would not be away much longer and Castillo might get curious.

He went through the small, barely furnished room. Soon he fastened his attentions to the desk and the padded chair in which Blind Sletter sat when he conducted matters of business.

So far, the Toff had only the slightest acquaintance with Sletter but he had heard rumours which had not even reached the ears of the police and his talk with Harry the Pug had riveted his attention on the Steam Packet.

The 'accident' which had befallen the writer of the maudlin letter had had its origin in the Toff's ingenious mind. The 'injured' waiter was already on his way to Spain, land of oranges and his birth, with his passage paid for by the Toff and enough money in his pockets to live idly for six months. The Toff believed in closing all gaps which might spring a leak.

For a full minute the Toff perched himself on the edge of the desk and stared at the padded chair. Unquestionably the secret rooms had ingress from Sletter's private parlour; he had seen Castillo, heavily laden, go into the room, to return empty-handed a quarter of an hour later.

But where did the hidden door lie?

The Toff leaned forward and pushed

43

against Sletter's chair. The control button, if there was one, would have to be handy for Blind Sletter while he was sitting at the desk and the chair was a likely spot.

It did not move when he pushed it. He exerted more force with the same result. The chair was fast to the floor.

Then he slipped off the table with his lips twisted wryly.

'Promising,' he told himself and ran his fingers quickly about the legs and arms of the chair. Nothing happened. Then he transferred his attentions to the desk. And, as he had expected, his finger rubbed over a slight protuberance.

'More promising,' he told himself.

Very carefully he pressed the knob—and in front of his eyes, so suddenly that he opened his lips in a mutter of surprise, two square yards of floor moved downwards with Sletter's chair in the centre of it.

The Toff released the button and pressed again and the patch slid upwards, joining the floor perfectly and noiselessly. No one could have guessed that it was a lift leading from Sletter's den to the secret rooms.

The Toff hesitated only for a second.

He had discovered what he had set out to find. If he went on, chancing Sletter's return or Castillo's curiosity, there was a likelihood of a very sticky end.

Unquestionably he should have waited.

Instead he felt the little bulge in his waist-band, which covered the life-preserver, and fingered the steel of the gun in his coat pocket. Then he sat in the chair and pressed the button.

Slowly the lift went down. For thirty seconds four blank walls slipped past him. Then the lift stopped, smooth and silent. In front of his eyes was a polished door.

The Toff took two short steps across the lift and tried the handle. It turned easily in his fingers which was what he had hoped. Then he went back, looking about him for the counterpart of the button which had controlled the upward movement of the lift. He found it, embedded in the frame-work of the door.

He grinned to himself.

'We know how it works,' he muttered. 'Now we'll see what else we can find.'

He pushed his right hand in his coat pocket, gripping his gun. Then he opened the door.

Had he been of a demonstrative nature he would have gasped at the sight in front of him. Here was a spacious lounge which would have done justice to a West End hotel. As he stepped forward his feet sank deep in thick pile carpet; looking round, he saw luxurious arm-chairs, shaded by palms, and in the far corner was a cocktail bar which made him lick his lips hopefully. The lounge was illuminated by wall lamps which sent a delicate blue light on the rich furnishings, soft, enchanting.

'Sletter can't see,' thought the Toff, 'but, by Hades, he knows what's what!'

He went farther into the lounge, nearly closing the door behind him. No one was there but a second door, opposite the first, was partly open and through it came the murmur of voices. One of them set the Toff's lips very tightly and his eyes were hard.

He had not been misinformed by Harry the Pug.

'So she will not talk, Garrotty.' The voice was soft, yet menacing, swaying with the strange cadence of the East. 'But there are ways in which we can make her.'

The Toff had expected developments when he had sat in Sletter's chair and slid downwards into the unknown; and that 'her' was the logical sequel to the shoe which he had found.

He had located the Lady of the Shoe and he felt pleased.

His eyes were harder still as he heard Dragoli's companion. 'You ain't gotta thing on makin' 'em talk, Dragoli. I got her so bad that she fainted right out. But she stayed dumb.' There was a reluctant admiration in the nasal twang of Mr Garrotty from Chicago. 'She's some dame, I'll say!'

Garrotty was facing the door as he spoke with Dragoli sitting in an easy chair opposite him. His face was of the basher type at the best of times. A livid scar ran across his right cheek from mouth to ear and his little eyes were screwed up evilly.

They opened to their widest when he saw the door on the other side of the room open slowly and the Toff slide through.

Garrotty cursed.

'What the hell—'

'So sorry to interrupt,' murmured the Toff, his voice honey-sweet. 'Carry on with what you were saying, Garrotty.'

Garrotty didn't carry on. His right hand went towards his pocket for a gun. But it stopped outside for the Toff's coat bulged suggestively.

'I shouldn't pull your gat,' he advised, walking easily into the room and pushing the door behind him. 'I've got one myself.' He smiled at Dragoli but his voice was like a lash. 'Good evening, Doctor. Quite a gathering of patients, isn't it? Not to say a meeting of friends.'

The Toff, ever honest with himself, admitted that there were points about Dragoli. The man did not turn a hair. As he leaned back, surveying the Toff, his sensuous lips parted.

'Keep quiet, Garrotty,' he said. 'This is a friend of ours.' And to the Toff: 'I hardly recognised you in your—uniform, Mr. Rollison.' The Toff laughed.

'You've only seen me once, Achmed, so I

47

won't blame you. That was when you potted my tyre—or Garrotty did—and'—he drawled the words irritatingly—'I found a lady's shoe. So I've come for the lady.'

'You know a lot of things,' said the Egyptian.

'You've just told me about her,' said the Toff gently. 'To borrow a phrase from Garrotty, where do you park the dame? Upstairs, downstairs or in my lady's chamber?'

He stopped, beaming about him.

Perhaps the Egyptian would never have answered the question. Perhaps Garrotty would have tried that bull-rush for the Toff which he was planning in his crafty mind. Perhaps the Toff would have made his last bow which was always possible in his little games.

But the question was answered in a manner which made the Toff's eyes soften for a moment, for all the fact that his lips tightened.

From a door on the right, half-way between the Toff and his enemies, came the girl.

Her body, usually slim and straight, was bent and drooping. Her eyes, a deep blue, were lack-lustre as she leaned against the door-post for support and stared.

And the Toff knew, as he saw her, that in the last few days she had been through hell itself. Thus it was not ignorance that made him say, before Dragoli spoke and before Garrotty cursed:

'Hallo, sweetheart! Walk right in and join

48

the party. We're all friends here, aren't we, Achmed?'

Anne Farraway moved towards him, sudden hope in her eyes.

CHAPTER FIVE

Quick Shooting

It was a very tricky situation. The Toff knew, as he looked at the two crooks with that mocking glint in his eye, that they were wishing him dead and in their own minds they were sure that he would never get out of the Steam Packet alive. But they didn't know the Toff. To him it was not so much a question of whether he would get away but when he would. There were many things that he wanted to learn, not a few of which he might find by bluffing the men who were facing him. Provided he had time.

None the less, the Toff knew that Garrotty had not come from the States unaccompanied; certain gentlemen with guns were probably within call. And there was the chance of interruption from Sletter or Castillo. Unquestionably it was a jam and he felt a little worried about getting out of the place with the girl, for her presence made it awkward.

Garrotty's third degree was not long past;

but the girl's chin went up as she realised just a little of what the Toff might mean.

So, as the Toff called her, she moved towards him.

It was too much for Garrotty. He swung on Dragoli.

'Why the hell don't you put him where he belongs, Dragoli? And make that dame keep still . . .'

The Toff smiled darkly.

'Steady, Yank,' he cautioned. 'There are two sides to this question now.'

The Yank was no fool and he knew that the little bump in the Toff's coat meant a gun; but he also knew that the gentlemen from Chicago were within call.

'Feeling better?' asked the Toff affably.

'You can start sayin' your prayers,' said Garrotty. And he called the girl by a foul name. 'Keep where you are, you—'

The Toff clucked his tongue against the roof of his mouth as he looked at Dragoli.

'Achmed, your American colleague doesn't seem to understand. He may have a gun but he can't reach it without losing an appreciable part of his fingers. Because I'm something of a marksman, though I say it as shouldn't. Tell him to calm down before I puncture his ribs. Then we can have the little chat I've been wanting.'

'You take the very words from my mouth,' said Dragoli suavely. His face was creased in a

50

smile which had all the cunning of the East in it and it did not deceive the Toff in the slightest. But it gave him time to think.

'Garrotty,' went on the Egyptian with a peremptory motion of his hand, 'won't offend again, my friend. And now, if I am not asking too much, what do you want?'

'The girl,' said the Toff amiably. 'I hated to think of her at your tender mercy, Achmed, so I came to take her away.'

It was bluff, of course, but Dragoli could not know how much truth there was in it. It was the beginning of what the Toff called psychological terrorism.

Dragoli took it well. His face was expressionless.

'And nothing else?' he asked.

'Lots of other things,' the Toff assured him calmly. 'You—and Garrotty—and . . .'

That 'and' was a masterpiece. It flowed from the Toff's lips and hung quivering in the air until the complacency of the Egyptian began to sag; which was exactly as the Toff intended.

'And,' he repeated, as though once was not enough 'those pals of yours with the music-hall name, Achmed. The Black Circle, don't they call themselves?'

The atmosphere seemed suddenly icy.

Dragoli hardly seemed to breathe.

From his silence the Toff learned what he wanted—that Dragoli was definitely an agent

51

of the Black Circle. The last thing in the world he had expected was to be taunted with it. It stupefied him and even made the sullen Garrotty uneasy.

The Toff saw the blazing eyes of the Egyptian, the thick lips of the gangster parted over broken teeth—and the girl, very near him now, staring in bewilderment. For the sensation which had been created was more like the consequences of an approaching earthquake than the slow voice of the Toff.

The Toff grinned, deciding that it was time to break the spell.

'It looks,' he drawled irritatingly, 'as though I've spilled the salt in the gravy. What's the trouble, Achmed?'

He wondered for a moment whether the Egyptian could keep back his rage and he moved the bulge in his pocket suggestively. It had a steadying effect.

'So you know about the Circle, do you?' breathed the Egyptian.

The Toff beamed.

'But you're smart. Not many men would have guessed that already.' He winked at the girl. 'Great minds are about us, Annabelle.'

And he said other things flippantly. Dragoli had confirmed what he had wanted to confirm—the complicity of the sinister Black Circle in the murder of Paul Goldman.

Dragoli spoke again, harping on the same chord.

'So—you know about the Black Circle. And you find it amusing?'

'Excruciatingly funny,' agreed the Toff.

'Goldman knew about it too,' the Egyptian said slowly. 'In fact, Goldman belonged to it. He was going to betray it, so he died.'

'Oh yes,' drawled the Toff. But if Dragoli's words left him cold, they had a different effect on the girl. The Toff saw the horror in her eyes and thought she would collapse.

'Steady,' he murmured and touched her arm. He felt her body quivering; mention of Goldman's death had broken her wonderful self-control.

Why?

The Toff was curious but this was no time for questions. For the moment the game was to bluff Dragoli into letting information slip.

He grinned.

'I shan't die,' he said easily. 'At least, not for a long time. I'm getting ready to leave you, Achmed.'

Dragoli's teeth showed.

'And your first step?' he demanded suavely.

'Safe refuge for Annabelle,' said the Toff, 'and then renewed hostilities, Achmed. Any suggestions?'

'What do you call—safe refuge?'

The Toff's smile was ridiculously smug.

'Scotland Yard, maybe, or a little cottage in the country. My dear Achmed, you've no idea how peaceful we can be in little old England—

53

outside the Steam Packet and the Black Circle.'

'And supposing,' demanded Dragoli, without rising to the bait, 'you don't get out of the Steam Packet?'

'Let's suppose something infinitely more pleasant,' suggested the Toff. 'Friends of mine, for instance, will be actively interested in the Steam Packet if I don't get out quite soon.'

'Ah!' muttered Dragoli, looking at the Toff doubtfully. Obviously he was wondering if that were true.

The Toff did not enlighten him.

'You see,' he pursued, 'our first meeting was accidental and you got the best of it. So I thought this one out first. Dragoli, said I to myself, must have been expecting me to call, otherwise he wouldn't have sent the spider the other day. He'll let me go because if he swats me he'll never learn how much I know, which would be a pity. And so—'

'Supposing I let you go?' asked Dragoli.

'There isn't any supposing about it,' said the Toff with great assurance. 'I'm going, Achmed, and I'm taking Annabelle with me.'

'And after that?'

'And after that,' said the Toff, who was under no delusions as to Dragoli's reason for prolonging the conversation and who was aware that Garrotty was moving backwards until he leaned against a door which probably possessed an electric button, 'it's just possible that you might give me best. But I'd be disappointed if you did. And just to lure you on, Achmed, I'll tell you that I don't know why you killed Goldman.'

Dragoli was quiet for a moment. So was Garrotty. The only sound that broke the silence was a low gasp from the girl.

The Toff stole a glance at her. Again the mention of Goldman broke through her self-control.

Dragoli's voice made the Toff forget her.

'No?' queried the Egyptian and there was a sharp edge to his voice for which the Toff had been waiting.

'But I shall find out,' said the Toff smoothly.

He was conscious of fresh tension in the air.

Dragoli's single 'no' had been a mistake for the change from suavity to hostility suggested that reinforcements were at hand. Garrotty's manner changed too. He moved a yard nearer the Toff, grinning. It was his first encounter, so he had an excuse.

'Clever, ain't yah, fella?'

'So clever,' murmured the Toff, 'that even you recognise it.' He looked at the girl. 'Annabelle, get right behind me and move towards the door. Don't take any notice of anything or anybody except me.'

Then he grinned at Dragoli, who was standing up.

'I shouldn't move if I were you. Funny things happen—like that!'

It came out of the blue or, more prosaically, from the Toff's gun. He had seen a leg poke out from a gap which had appeared suddenly in the wall and fired from his pocket. The shot echoed loudly as the bluish flame spat—and the leg disappeared, amidst cursing.

'First blood,' smiled the Toff and laughed at the sudden rage in Dragoli's face. 'I warned you, Achmed. This isn't a plaything and I've used it before.'

He dropped his voice so that only the girl just behind him heard his words.

'Open the door. Cut across the lounge and get in the lift. Count a hundred and if I'm not out by then, press the button you'll see on a level with your eyes and when you get to the top yell for a policeman. OK?'

'Yes,' she said and the Toff liked the quiet assurance of her voice. She was more self-possessed now.

He saw Garrotty rushing towards him like a great bull, fists whirling like flails. He saw a second pair of legs inserting themselves through the sliding wall. He saw the glint of steel in Dragoli's hands.

His gun spoke. Dragoli raised his hand with a gasp and the gun clattered to the floor. Blood dropped from the Egyptian's shattered fingers.

'I warned you,' he said and his gun spoke again. The bullet whistled past Garrotty's head, making the man flinch back—it was a

56

lucky thing, the Toff thought at that moment, that he had caught Garrotty at a time when the gangster couldn't get at his gun—and embedded itself in the thigh of a second man who was climbing through the hole in the wall. The man staggered back, face distorted with fury and pain.

'Cheer up, Handsome,' taunted the Toff. 'That was only a taster. Now for the real thing—'

For Garrotty was on him. The Toff heard the hiss of the Yank's harsh breathing, saw a fist like a leg of mutton shoot out, covered with a brass knuckle-duster.

The Toff stepped lightly to one side and Garrotty's hand hummed past him. The Toff's fist jabbed out—and Garrotty felt as though an elephant had kicked him in the tender part of the neck.

'That's for puncturing my tyre,' muttered the Toff.

Garrotty grunted, shaking his great head. He went back a pace then lunged with his foot. As the foot swept up, the Toff saw Dragoli standing by the table holding another gun in his uninjured left hand.

The Toff ducked and swerved at the same time. A bullet whistled over his head and plonked into the wall. Garrotty's knee swept in front of his eyes.

The Toff shot out his hand and gripped the gangster's kneecap. He twisted hard, the harder as Garrotty snorted with agony and swayed helpessly on one leg, then the Toff loosened his hold and shot up a pile-driver which caught his man on the point of the jaw. Garrotty rocketed backwards, thudding to the floor.

'That,' murmured the Toff, 'is for what you did to Annabelle. And there's more to come.'

His eyes swept round the room. Dragoli was finding it difficult to control his gun in his left hand and his right arm hung at his side. Garrotty was reaching for the gun on the floor. A third man was climbing through the hidden panel in the wall.

'Time to go,' the Toff told himself.

With a smooth speed which startled all who came in contact with him he slipped backwards, out of the room. Banging the door to, he grabbed the back of a heavy arm-chair and overturned it. On the instant something thudded on the other side and rattled against it, taptap-tap, tap-tap-tap, remorseless, ominous!

A machine-gun was in harness, which was what the Toff had expected and why he had been discreet.

'Not today, baker,' he said cheerfully, for he was very pleased with himself.

In the lounge Anne Farraway was waiting, tense with fear. The gunfire on the other side of the door made her more afraid. Already the panels of the door were sagging and splintering under the fusillade.

The Toff reached her and smiled encouragingly.

'Quick's the word, young lady. Achmed and the boys are getting crosser every minute and Garrotty's too full for words.'

He stepped into the lift and pressed the control button. The cage moved upwards, tantalisingly slow. Before they were out of sight the man and the girl saw the wood of the door give way and a hail of lead spatter across the lounge.

The girl's breath came fast. The Toff knew that she was thinking of what would have happened had they been down there, helpless against the shooting. He cheered her up.

'Trouble isn't trouble, cherub, until it gets you in the middle. Sletter and the folk upstairs are out. Once we're up top we'll be in the street in two ticks and all the machine-guns in Chicago won't hurt us. How are you feeling?'

Anne Farraway made a big effort.

'Fine,' she said and smiled.

'I'll say you are!' breathed the Toff.

He smiled at her, seeing the flurry of auburn hair about her forehead and the deep blue of her eyes. A deep sense of satisfaction filled him.

Then he put her out of his immediate thoughts and wondered what would happen when the lift reached Sletter's office. He handled his gun—just for safety, he told Anne.

But their luck held. The office, sliding gradually into view, was as empty as when the Toff had first entered it.

He hopped out of the lift before it stopped, helped the girl out and, putting his hand to her elbow, propelled her towards the door. He touched the handle.

'The last barrier,' he said with a smile.

The door opened easily. Outside, the passage was empty.

'Through the kitchen and home, little one. And then you can tell all your troubles to Uncle Richard.'

Which might have seemed optimistic but he had little fear of trouble from the kitchen staff. And he was justified. A cook and a maid goggled and he waved his hand to them. A waiter started to speak but the Toff snapped his fingers in his face.

The next thing Anne Farraway saw was a stretch of York Road, a tram and a policeman. Somehow the Toff got her into a taxi and settled her in a corner.

'You're a very good girl,' he said. 'And I believe I've a shoe which might be yours.'

CHAPTER SIX

Anne's Story

Rollison, helped by an outraged Jolly, prepared the spare room at the flat to accommodate Anne. It was not surprising that the girl was in a state of collapse. Her eyes were widely dilated and her slim body trembled. Dangerously near hysteria, thought Rollison, and called in a doctor who diagnosed fatigue and severe nervous strain.

Is she well enough to be questioned?' demanded Rollison. The two men were in the drawing-room of the flat while Anne was in bed in the spare room.

'Certainly not.' The doctor was emphatic. 'If she's worried there is a strong likelihood of complete breakdown, mental and physical. I'll give her a draught and look in in the morning. A good night's rest might alter things completely.'

'Hum,' said Rollison. 'Does that go for the police too?'

The medico suppressed a natural curiosity.

It goes for anyone, Mr. Rollison. It would be a criminal act to awaken her when she was sleeping off the effect of the draught.' The speaker chuckled dryly. 'But it would take an earthquake to disturb her.'

A curious little smile hovered about the Toff's lips as he walked with the medico to the door.

'Thanks,' he said. 'Make it a real strong one, doc, and don't be surprised if you get a summons from Scotland Yard. They never seem to believe what I tell 'em.'

Forty minutes later the Toff left Anne, already sleeping soundly. By way of precaution he had hired, by telephone, two ex-pugilists who arrived promptly from a nearby gymnasium and left them to entertain Jolly, just in case of trouble. But somehow the Toff did not expect things to happen very quickly.

He went to Scotland Yard and had no trouble in getting to McNab. The Chief Inspector welcomed him soberly into his small office which, apart from the detective's chair, was devoid of ordinary creature comforts.

The Toff squatted on the corner of an untidy desk.

'Well?' queried McNab stolidly. He was a permanently stolid individual.

'I've just had a fight,' confessed the Toff who had changed into an immaculate evening dress and was at his spotless best.

McNab grunted.

'That isna' unusual.'

'Sure and it isn't,' agreed the Toff pleasantly. 'But there was something different about this one, Mac. I smote Garrotty the Yank on the Adam's apple and he's trying to get his swallow back.'

McNab was interested but he stayed stolid.

'So ye're still nosin' around that, are ye?'

'Not half,' admitted the Toff.

He related, without embellishments, the affair of the tarantula which was enough to make any man nose around anything. Then, eyeing the Scot very closely, he confessed his suspicions of the Steam Packet. That he had followed them up, that things had happened and what they were.

McNab was very still for a while. Then:

'So ye had Garrotty and Dragoli cornered—and ye let them go?'

'It might be said,' murmured the Toff modestly, 'that I got away, Mac.'

McNab bit off the end of a black cigar.

'Ye should 'a' told us about the Steam Packet,' he said quietly, 'before ye went there.'

The Toff admitted that there was some justification in that view-point. But he noticed, with considerable interest, that McNab was not so indignant about it as he might have been. It suggested that the detective was very nearly glad that the Toff had not forced the police to take precipitate action and raid Sletter's place. The Toff, realising this, assumed that the police had a plan of campaign.

He took a shot in the dark.

'Of course I should,' he drawled. 'But I knew you wouldn't want Dragoli and the

Yank—yet. You're after'—his voice went very soft—'you're after the Black Circle, aren't you, Mac?'

Just as, a few hours before, tension had suddenly sprung into the secret rooms of the Steam Packet, so did the atmosphere of the small office go still.

McNab's hand stopped half-way between his mouth and the desk, grey smoke curled upwards from the motionless cigar.

'And so,' he said at last, 'ye really know about that?'

The Toff shrugged.

'I know it exists, old soldier, but I can't tell you much more than that. It's been about for a long time, I imagine. And the Goldman murder was part of it.'

McNab spent a long time examining the ash of his cigar. He was a very cautious man and the Toff waited patiently to see how he reacted to the challenge. McNab could turn nasty: which would make it very awkward for the Toff. Or, as had happened before, he might become communicative and end up with an offer of co-operation.

The detective reached his decision. He pulled open the drawer of his desk and took out a small packet about the size of a matchbox which was carefully wrapped in brown paper. One end was sealed but the other had been opened and tucked in again.

McNab flicked the little packet across the

desk and it came to rest a couple of inches from the Toff's hand.

'Take a look at that,' said the Scot.

The Toff picked the packet up, untucked the opened end and squinted inside. He saw what he had expected to see when McNab had first shown him the packet—a fine white powder. Then the Toff wetted the end of his little finger, dabbed the powder and then tasted it gingerly.

He pulled a wry face.

'So,' he said finally and his voice was very hard, 'that's it. Snow.'

'Aye,' agreed McNab, equally grim. 'Snow.'

For cocaine or, in the vernacular, 'snow,' was the worst evil against which the police had to fight. Other crimes could be traced to a single source and their effect was comparatively small. But the effect of dope-trafficking was insidious, never-ending, wrecking men and women, turning them from decent citizens into social outcasts.

And snow was raising its ugly head in London again. The Black Circle was distributing it.

The Toff asked a question, although he knew the answer before it came.

'Is it in big quantities?'

'The City's flooded with it—overnight, almost,' McNab said. 'We've been well on top of the situation for months and then it got out of hand before we knew where we were. There had been rumours—we sent a man to Stamboul to try and find out something. But it's burst on us verra quick.'

The Toff swung his legs.

'The whisper came from Goldman?' he suggested.

'Aye,' said McNab. 'We had a note from him on the morning of his death, saying there was snow about, that he knew where it was and how much would it be worth if he squealed? There was no address, of course, so we couldn't trace him.'

'Of course not,' murmured the Toff.

'Mind you,' said McNab, 'we knew the Black Circle was behind it. Ninety per cent of the dope on the continent comes from Stamboul— the Circle's headquarters. What we didn't know was who was running it over here.'

'And Goldman could have told you,' murmured the Toff. 'Dragoli killed Goldman to stop him from squealing. Find Dragoli and you've got your man.'

'Too easy,' grunted McNab but there was a gleam of humour in his eyes. 'We could have got Dragoli twenty-four hours ago, Rolleeson. But that's not enough.' The Scot leaned forward and banged his fist on the desk. 'Where does Dragoli get the stuff? How does he get it into the country? Where does he keep it? That's what we're after, Rolleeson.'

The Toff swung his legs.

'And your game is to trail Achmed, is it?'

McNab seemed ashamed of his little outburst.

'Just that,' he admitted. And he smiled lugubriously. 'That's why I'm not sorry you've made them worry about getting away from Lambeth. They'll clear out, without thinking that the police know anything about 'em, but we'll be on their tail.'

'I see,' murmured the Toff, lighting a cigarette.

Many of the mysteries were cleared away and up to a point the affair read like an open book. Goldman had been a member of the Black Circle and had seen a means of making capital out of his knowledge as well as gaining immunity from the police. Dragoli, who was flooding London with dope, had discovered the treachery and killed Goldman, hiring Garrotty and his gunmen so as to keep the trail away from himself.

But Dragoli was not out of the woods by a long way. Something had gone radically wrong with his plans. The Toff, who knew nothing of Goldman's dying taunt—'It's on paper—in black and white'—guessed that the Egyptian believed that the girl held the key to the mystery.

Otherwise why had Garrotty been trying to make her talk?

The Toff puffed smoke out slowly. Then he slid off the edge of the table and walked slowly across the office floor.

'Well,' he said quietly, 'I'm not saying that you don't stand a chance of getting what you want, Mac. But there's one thing that's worrying you—'

McNab scowled.

'What do ye mean?'

'The girl,' said the Toff gently.

And, as he had expected, the Scot's eyes narrowed.

'Yes,' he admitted. 'I'm worried about her.' He stared suspiciously at the Toff's bland countenance. 'What are ye getting at, Rolleeson?'

The Toff grinned.

'Just this,' he said smoothly. 'When I came away from the Steam Packet I had the girl with me, Mac. Steady, steady now'—he held up his hand as McNab started to interrupt—'don't be too hasty. I brought her with me and she's at my flat. But she's in a bad way. In fact, a well-known doctor, whose word you'll have to take, forbids anything in the way of excitement until the morning at least. So we've to hold our fire until then.'

'I'm not so sure about that,' McNab said waspishly.

The Toff leaned over and scribbled on a scrap of paper in front of the detective's nose.

'There's the doctor's name and his telephone number. Ring him up or go and see him. And'—the Toff's smile was expansive— 'put a couple of men outside the house to make sure I don't elope with her, Mac. Then trot along yourself in the morning. Say elevenish.'

Which, after a telephone call and much demur, the Chief Inspector promised to do. If he could have seen twenty-four hours into the future he would have made a much greater demur!

*   *   *

The Toff was draped—no other word fits the pose—about a deep arm-chair in the sitting-room of his flat. His eyes were half-closed and from the corner of his shapely mouth drooped a cigarette. His forehead was unruffled and his eyes were gleaming. A presentable young man.

Anne Farraway thought so, as she saw him at her leisure for the first time. It was hard to picture him, gun in hand, keeping Garrotty and Dragoli at bay, laughing at the murder in their eyes. Yet it was he, beyond question.

The Toff smiled at Anne lazily. She had only just come into the room and she was a rare sight. It amazed the Toff, so far as he was capable of amazement, that she should have recovered from the effect of her ordeal so quickly.

'Breakfast in ten minutes,' drawled the Toff. 'Did you sleep well?'

Anne nodded and stretched her slim legs in front of her luxuriously.

'Almost,' she said, 'as though I'd been drugged.'

There was a twinkle in the Toff's eyes.

'A spot of veronal in your glass of milk, young lady, on medical advice. Feeling better for it?'

She nodded.

Her eyes, very, very blue, were brimming over with what the pedant calls gratitude and her mouth, which was Cupid-bowed and soft, was trembling. She had a dimple, the Toff noticed when she smiled, on either cheek.

The look of her made him very satisfied with life. For, in the rig-out which he had borrowed from an obliging friend, Anne Farraway looked delightfully trim and neat. The clothes did nothing to emphasise the clearness of her skin now that she was rested, nor the determined lines of her mouth and chin; they were emphatic enough. Her hair, which the Toff had noticed in Sletter's lift, was dark brown, wavy and luxuriant. She was very lovely.

She was very grateful. It seemed a dream, the manner in which the Toff had spirited her away from the rooms at the Steam Packet—a pleasant dream, after the nightmare of her interrogation at Garrotty's hands.

After breakfast, which was a complete success, she told the Toff about that. Of Garrotty, threatening, shouting, his thugs leering, cursing, banging clappers in her ears, insistently, maddeningly, shooting question after question, prodding her, keeping her from sleeping for forty-eight dreadful hours, driving her mad—mad!

'I'm almost sorry,' the Toff said when she had finished, 'that I didn't kill Garrotty while I had the chance. But perhaps it's as well.'

He smiled at her, seeing the hint of horror which had crept into her eyes from the memory of her ordeal. He wished that he could keep her away from all thought of the affair until it was all over. But that was impossible. If she knew anything the police would have to be told and the Toff, with all respect to McNab, believed that he could talk to her more gently than the burly detective.

He lit a cigarette slowly.

'Well,' he said softly, 'what was it all about, Annabelle?'

She took a deep breath.

'I suppose I'll have to tell you,' she said in a voice only just above a whisper.

'Me, or someone else, and it had better be me,' murmured Rollison.

She was silent for a minute and he realised that she was forcing herself to be calm.

'First,' she said at last, 'I'd better tell you this: Goldman is not the name of the man who was murdered. His true name was—Farraway. My brother.'

The Toff kept quiet and still. His heart was full of pity. No wonder she hated the mention

71

of Goldman's name and of his death.

Anne Farraway went on:

'Of course, I know he wasn't all that he should have been. John was always looking for something to do with a kick in it. He got mixed up with the wrong set soon after he left school. He was sentenced to five years' penal servitude. That'—her voice was barely audible—'smashed all of us up. I mean, my mother and step-father. Mother died a little while afterwards and Father never seemed to recover from the shock. We—we drifted apart. And'—there was a firmness in her voice as she went on—'I was glad that Mother had gone, because John was harder—worse than ever he had been. He went abroad after working with my step-father for a few months. I only heard from him now and again when he sent me money.'

She stopped for a moment and Rollison thought of the queer contradictions in a man's make-up. John Farraway had been one of the worst men but even when he had been operating for the Black Circle he had sent money regularly to his sister. He wondered who the step-father had been but decided not to press the girl for information.

Anne went on suddenly, almost as if she had read Rollison's thoughts.

'I couldn't touch the money,' she said with spirit. 'I put it in the bank, under his name, and managed to get a job in one of the

Chelmsford estate offices. I lived—I still live there—in a little cottage three miles away from the town. Then, just over a week ago, John came back.'

Anne paused again and leaned back in her chair. Rollison was content to wait.

'I knew he was afraid of something,' continued the girl, 'but he wouldn't say what it was. He was in need of money, and grateful for the account in the bank, but said it wasn't enough, that he knew how he could get big money quickly and get out of England again—to somewhere a long way from Turkey.

'There was nothing I could do to dissuade him. I gave up trying and hoped that he would settle down. But on the next day—it was late and I had only been home a few minutes because I'd been to a dance in Chelmsford—he was waiting for me, with a car that he had hired, and he said that he had to get up to London quickly. I had to go with him because, he said, it would be safer for him. I didn't try to stop him. He was too nervy, afraid of something—somebody. Who it was I didn't know until we were stopped on the road. Then I saw Dragoli for the first time.'

For a third time Anne stopped and Rollison stood up and went towards her, sitting on the arm of her chair and resting his hand lightly on her shoulder.

'Steady,' he said. 'It's all over, remember.'

He felt her body shaking.

73

'Yes,' she said heavily, 'I suppose it is. Well—John saw Dragoli and was terrified. He stopped the car and whispered to me, almost frantically. 'Get away,' he said; 'get away and go to Scotland Yard. Tell them the man who is selling the snow is Dragoli and that everything that matters is on the plan fastened in the strap of your left shoe!'

The Toff's body went rigid. The significance of the information made him gasp. All that mattered was fastened in the strap of the girl's shoe—the shoe which he had found on the road amid the wreckage.

For three days and more he had had the solution of the riddle slung in a drawer of his wardrobe.

'I tried to get away,' went on Anne lifelessly, 'but Garrotty came after me. I struggled and in the struggle I lost my left shoe. Where it is now I don't know. And'—her voice grew firmer—'I'm glad I don't. If I knew I think I would have told Dragoli—it was awful to keep silent while they were pestering me, questioning me. But I had to because I'd no more idea where the shoe was than Adam.'

Anne stopped and leaned back in her chair. The Toff kept his hand on her shoulder for a moment then took it away and stood up from the arm of the chair. He went in front of her, a smile hovering about the corners of his mouth.

'You're a great kid,' he said. 'Were you happy in your country cottage?'

'Yes,' said Anne, 'very happy. I'm hoping to get married soon and settle down there.'

'Splendid,' smiled the Toff. 'Count me in if you need a best man! And now'—his smile was tempered with seriousness—'be prepared for excitement. You remember the shot which was fired out of the Daimler when Garrotty and Dragoli were taking you away?'

Anne caught her breath.

'Yes. I was afraid someone else had been hurt.'

'No such luck for dear Achmed,' drawled the Toff. 'I was in the other car and I ducked in time. Also I found your shoe.'

Anne's looked at him incredulously, then leaned forward.

'You found it? And you've still got it?'

'I have,' said the Toff with assurance. 'Hold on a minute while I get it.'

He went out of the room with a shrewd idea as to what would be found in the strap of the shoe. He smiled faintly at the irony of fate; all the time he had been sitting on the solution of McNab's worries—the secret hang-out of Dragoli, the place where the supplies of cocaine were kept.

Within three minutes he was back. The girl stood up, tense with excitement.

'That's it,' she said quickly. 'That's my shoe!'

'You can bet your sweet life it is,' said the Toff. 'In the strap, eh? Where's my penknife?'

As he spoke he rooted in his pockets for the knife; a minute later he had cut through the stitches of the strap—on inspection it was obvious that they had been made by an amateur with a needle—and a smile of sheer satisfaction dawned as he took out a thin spill of paper.

Anne gasped, her eyes bright with excitement.

'The bag of tricks,' murmured the Toff and uncoiled the paper.

If Anne, peering over his shoulder, was a trifle disappointed at the ink-drawn sketch, the Toff was greatly pleased. It was a plan, not drawn to scale but accurate enough for the purpose, of the situation of Dragoli's drug warehouse.

Once this place was raided, the back of the drug traffic would be broken.

'Do you recognise the place?' asked the girl.

The Toff was tracing along one line which was intersected at various points by two small parallel lines. He realised that it represented the river Thames with the intersections representing bridges. He transferred his attention to the several straight lines, all converging to one spot which was marked in a black square. And beneath the black square were the words:

RED LION

The Toff's lips formed a soundless whistle.

'Well, I'm damned and benighted!' he exclaimed after a pregnant pause. 'The Red Lion—Harry the Pug's place! The little swab double-crossed me after all.

Anne caught something of his excitement.

'You know it?'

'Know it!' The Toff's eyes were very bright. 'I should say I do! It's bang on the Thames— the stuff could be taken from a ship into the Red Lion inside five minutes. And if there was a scare, Dragoli could be out of the place in a jiffy, taking most of the dope with him.' The Toff looked into Anne's eyes and chuckled. 'It's a shame but McNab will have the time of his life when he gets this!'

'And there isn't any chance of Dragoli getting away?'

'Not a ghost of a chance,' said the Toff with superb optimism. 'But there's likely to be a rough-house down at the Red Lion before it's over.' He eased his collar, feeling hot and sticky. 'You know, I'm getting warm with the thought of it.'

Anne stood up and walked towards the window.

It's hot in here,' she said. 'I think there's a storm brewing.'

'There is,' the Toff said with assurance. 'A big one, too.'

CHAPTER SEVEN

The Toff Slips Up

Perhaps it has not been sufficiently stressed in this story of one of the Toff's biggest adventures that he, like all men, was human.

He had seen, with a clarity of vision which was almost uncanny, the possibilities of the situation. He had discovered the Steam Packet, had made it too hot for Garrotty and Dragoli and now he believed that there would be a breathing-space while the Egyptian conferred with his masters on the next move. So the Toff had sent the two hired pugs away for he was not expecting trouble.

To do them justice, the police were. McNab had placed the two plain-clothes men in the vicinity of the Toff's flat and they had been watching for hours. The Toff noticed them when he went to the open window to get a breath of air. The thunder which was brewing made the room hot and stuffy but by the window it was fresher, as it had need to be.

He pointed the watchers out to Anne.

'Perhaps,' he said flippantly, 'McNab thinks I'll spirit you away before he comes with his questions.'

'Are you going to?' asked Anne.

'Not yet,' said the Toff. He eased his collar.

'It really is hot in here.'

It was. He put it down to the thunder that was threatening and therein made a grave mistake.

Unknown to him and to the police, the second-floor flat in the house adjacent to the Toff—a corner house—had been recently let, and let furnished. The new tenants had, in point of fact, been in possession for two days—even before the affair at the Steam Packet. And they were in the flat while the Toff talked with Anne Farraway—which accounted largely for the stuffiness of the room.

The very effort of thinking seemed to tire the Toff and he put this down off-handedly to the break in the tension, now that he knew the truth. He wiped his damp forehead with a silk handkerchief and grinned at Anne.

'It wouldn't be any hotter,' he said, 'in the place where Garrotty's going. Joke.'

Anne smiled obediently. She felt more like smiling now than she had done for a long time. The Toff inspired confidence—and she lacked his suspicious mind which was just as well.

All that had to be done was to take the plan to the police.

The Toff smiled as she said as much.

'I suppose you're right, sweet one. I've looked everywhere I can and I don't see the catch. I've to potter round to McNab—in fact he'll be calling soon and that'll save trouble—and hand the whole thing over to him.

Whether Garrotty and Dragoli fall into his hands is a matter of conjecture. But there'll be the merry hell of a scrap—that's a safe bet.'

He levered himself out of his chair. The end of the Black Circle's English campaign was in sight and the Toff was very pleased.

Then he frowned. There was something the matter, something which had not happened to him in all the years of his life, except in those days when he had run the hundred in a shade over evens and he was trying to find a reason.

He failed. But the fact remained that his heart was thumping against his breast and he was breathing hard.

'I'm puffed,' he said slowly and looked at Anne questioningly. 'Do you feel all right?'

The strangeness of his manner worried her.

'Yes. I feel warm, that's all.'

'Very warm,' agreed the Toff. 'Much too warm.'

An unpleasant thought was forming in his mind. It made him feel cold, in spite of the heat and the stickiness of his body. Little beads of perspiration were standing out on his forehead—and the palms of his hands were greasy with sweat.

'I don't believe,' he thought constrictedly, 'that I've fallen for poison. I . . .'

But he felt a terrible conviction that somehow he had, that somehow the Black Circle had reached him.

He thought back on the food that Jolly had

prepared but his thoughts were muddled.

Nothing was clear.

He walked slowly towards the telephone, looking at Anne, seeing the strain about her eyes. She was breathing hard and with increasing difficulty.

The smile which he flashed towards her was a mockery.

'We'd better—tell—the police about the plan,' he said carefully. He heard the pauses between the words as though he was listening to someone else speaking from a long way off.

The telephone, on a table near the window, looked a black blur. He wondered whether he would be able to speak coherently, then thought muzzily of the detectives outside. Perhaps it would be better to signal to them.

His fingers touched the telephone but slipped along the shiny surface. He managed to get the earpiece off its hook and tried hard to set his lips to the microphone, for he knew that he would never reach the window. His legs were wobbling—his arms went stiff.

His mind was just a mad medley. Nothing ran normally, nothing looked normal. Anne, struggling against the unseen horror in the room, looked a hundred miles away.

Then the room whirled crazily about him. The floor seemed to sway in front of his eyes; a roaring thunder filled his ears. He tried to speak—to shout—but the words were but a gurgle at the back of his throat.

Then everything went black. He fell heavily to the floor.

Anne Farraway tried to scream but something caught at her throat. She tried to move but her limbs were stiff. She saw, horrified, the still body of the Toff, the telephone—off its hook but useless—and then she too felt the room swirling about her and she dropped into a yawning oblivion.

*   *   *

In the newly tenanted flat next to the Hon Richard Rollison's, two men stood close together, peering through a small hole drilled in the wall. They saw the whole drama as they watched in silence.

Garrotty was holding a long gas-cylinder with its nozzle inserted in a second hole in the wall. Through the hole the poison crept insidiously, striking the Toff and the girl into unconsciousness.

Dragoli was standing next to Garrotty. He turned away suddenly.

'That is enough,' he said smoothly. 'Stop the gas, Garrotty. The quicker we get them out of there the better.'

Garrotty turned off the gas control of the cylinder and swung round quickly enough. Sight of the plan which the Toff had found in the girl's shoe had made him uneasy. It had been a narrow shave. If the police had found it first, a hundred policemen would have been in the neighbourhood of the Red Lion within an hour. And Garrotty did not like the idea of being caught red-handed in the dope racket in England.

'Sure,' he grunted. 'What about Rollison's servant?'

Dragoli snapped at him.

'You've got a silencer on your gun, haven't you, and those two pugs have gone.'

'Sure,' repeated Garrotty placatingly. 'I was only asking.'

'Then hurry!' ordered Dragoli, leading the way to the kitchen quarters of the flat.

A door opened from the kitchen to a small square of iron grid which was part and parcel of the emergency exit at the rear of the houses. The fact that Dragoli's temporary habitation was a corner house made it easy to get Rollison and the girl into his own flat for the Toff's kitchen door opened on to the same landing. After that it was only a question of getting the couple down the front stairs and into the car which was waiting outside. Dragoli did not mean the man or the girl to live for a minute after he had got them to the Red Lion for the Pug would handle their bodies, would be prepared to work more freely now there was no fear of the Toff.

Garrotty went out of the kitchen first. His right hand, in his pocket, was fastened round a gun. He lounged across the iron landing carelessly then opened the Toff's back door with his left hand.

Jolly was bending over the gas-stove. He looked round with a start of surprise and his mouth opened.

'Just keep your trap shut,' warned Garrotty and showed his gun.

Jolly's eyes widened. He backed away, his hands in front of his face. He hardly saw the gangster's hand flash out before the butt of the gun crashed on his forehead.

Jolly dropped down, a queer gurgle in his throat.

Dragoli pushed past the American towards the inner door. He jerked it open with his left hand—his right hand was wrapped in bandages, the result of the Toff's shooting.

'The girl first,' said the Egyptian.

In a trice both men were across the small hall and in the Toff's sitting-room. The Toff was lying by the table, on his back and breathing stertorously. Anne Farraway was in a huddled heap three yards away from him.

'You take her,' said Dragoli. 'I will drag Rollison towards the door.'

Garrotty picked the girl up and swayed towards the door, carrying her with hardly an effort, her limp form over his shoulder. He was on the landing outside before Dragoli had pulled the Toff as far as the first door.

And then the Egyptian heard something which made him loosen his hold of the Toff and dart towards the window. It was the sound of a high-powered car which drew up outside the house.

The murmur of voices floated upwards. One a gruff, authoritative voice.

Is everything all right up there?'

'Nobody's been out, sir,' came the answer.

'Good.'

Dragoli stared out of the window, hidden from view by the curtains. He saw Chief Inspector McNab stepping out of his car and saw one of the watching detectives draw near him.

Dragoli swung round, darting his left hand to his pocket for a gun. The Toff would have to be left behind—but it would be a dead Toff.

The Egyptian cursed again for the gun wasn't there. He had taken it from his pocket in the next-door flat and the chance was gone.

He thought once of smashing a chair on the Toff's skull but it would take time. McNab's heavy footsteps were on the stairs. In less than half a minute the detective would be outside the door.

Dragoli stepped over the Toff's prostrate body and sped along to the kitchen. It was a matter of seconds now. He heard the policeman's heavy tread on the top stair and a sudden gasp of consternation.

McNab had seen the Toff.

Garrotty appeared suddenly on the landing and the Yank's eyes widened at the fear on

Dragoli's face.

'What's up, boss?'

'The police!' hissed Dragoli. 'Get down to the car.'

Again the position of the house—on the corner—was invaluable. The car, with a uniformed chauffeur sitting at the wheel and the inert body of Anne Farraway lolling back in the rear seat, was outside. The watching detectives had seen it but being in a different street it had not occurred to them that it was concerned with the Toff.

One of them heard its engine whirring but a second later was startled out of his wits by McNab's stentorian bellow from the window of the Toff's flat.

'Simpson, blow your whistle! Get round the corner!'

The detective jerked into motion. He saw the big car—a Daimler—sliding along the kerb and with a sudden flash of intuition realised what it meant. He broke into a run.

McNab saw him and swung round, cursing. If he had been five minutes earlier he would have arrived in time.

With a speed surprising in so heavy a man, the Chief Inspector raced down the stairs and burst into the street. The police car was already on the move and he jumped into it, rapping instructions to a policeman who was hurrying along the road, summoned by Simpson's whistle. Farther down the street a second whistle blared. Footsteps thudded on the pavement.

'Get a doctor up there!' snapped McNab to the patrolman and thudded into the seat next to the driver. 'After them, James—drive like the devil!'

The engine roared and the police car swung round the corner. Detective Simpson made a flying leap for it, caught the door and managed to open it. He dropped back in the seat.

McNab screwed his head round.

'Use the radio,' he ordered. Instruct all police cars to follow the blue Daimler, number double X seven-three-five-four-one, and police car seventeen.' He turned round to the driver. 'Is that Daimler number right?'

The driver nodded. He had just been able to get the number as the police car had swerved round the corner. By now Dragoli's Daimler was a hundred yards away, racing along the road at a frantic speed. The pursuing police car would never overtake it unless there was a traffic block.

But McNab was not worried about that. In a dozen places police cars and Flying Squad cars were looking out for the blue Daimler, helped by the directions which Simpson radioed second by second. Unless the Daimler was lost somewhere in the rabbit-warrens of the East End, it would never get away. The police net was closing round it.

*   *   *

The Toff was sprawling across his bed when he came to and his first sensation was a violent pain in his stomach. He lay back gasping for a minute while the pain gradually dulled. Then he struggled into a sitting position, feeling a firm hand on his arm.

'Steady,' said a quiet voice. 'Don't overdo it.'

He managed a feeble grin. He felt as though every atom of strength had been drained from him and the thought of overdoing anything was bitterly ironic.

He looked into the face of the man who was bending over him and grinned again.

'Hullo, Doc! Getting quite good friends, aren't we?'

The doctor, who had attended Anne Farraway on the previous evening, smiled grimly. He had pumped a restorative into the Toff's arm but only at the urgent request of the tall iron-grey man who was standing by the window, staring anxiously at the Toff.

The Toff saw the man and frowned. He recognised him vaguely but his mind was cloudy—nothing seemed clear. He could not even remember what had been happening.

Then he saw something in the iron-grey man's hands and a flash of understanding went through his mind. The grin left his face. For the man was holding a shoe and the Toff remembered what had been in the shoe.

He recognised the stranger too. It was Sir Ian Warrender, an Assistant Commissioner of Police at Scotland Yard.

Warrender took a step towards him.

'Did you get 'em?' asked the Toff.

'No,' said Warrender and his voice was harsh. 'We lost them in Shadwell. McNab's hunting through the docks.'

The Toff slid off the bed and his expression was grim. He waved the doctor aside.

'I'm all right,' he said briefly. 'Thanks.' He looked at Warrender. 'Dragoli's gone to earth at the Red Lion, and I know the way to the place blindfold. Is your car outside?'

The Assistant Commissioner smiled grimly.

'There are three cars outside,' he said, 'with a full complement of men, waiting for you to come round.'

The Toff was at the door.

'Let's get to them,' he said laconically. 'And if Dragoli's hurt that girl I'll tear him to pieces!'

CHAPTER EIGHT

Trouble At The Red Lion

The three police cars tore through London towards the East End. The Toff was at the wheel of the leading car with Sir Ian Warrender sitting next to him. Behind them they could hear the tapping of the radio signals which were being flashed.

'All police cars meet at Red Lion, Shadwell. All cars to radio arrival and situation at Red Lion.'

Time and time again the message went out. Every few minutes the Assistant Commissioner turned in his seat to see if there was any message from other cars. The operator, sitting upright with the earphones pressed close to his head, made no signal at first.

The Toff, his eyes on the road in front of him, zigzagging the powerful police car, was not thinking of the radio messages. He was thinking of Anne Farraway in Dragoli's hands and the thought of what that Eastern degenerate might do to her made him writhe.

The car was roaring along the Mile End Road when Warrender, radio at his ear, touched the Toff's arm.

'Well?' The Toff missed the tail-board of a

lorry by a hair-breadth. Warrender's voice was thin with excitement.

'McNab's at the Red Lion with a dozen men,' he said. 'They're raiding now.'

'That's fine,' said the Toff. He put the car between the kerb and a moving tram. A hundred yards ahead lay the turning which he would take to get to the Red Lion. More than anything else, he wanted to be in at the death.

Then Warrender spoke again.

'There's been shooting,' he muttered hoarsely. 'The Red Lion's barricaded. McNab's drawn away.'

The Toff said nothing but his eyes were hard. Those terse sentences carried a picture to his mind with startling clarity. He could almost see the dingy building of Harry the Pug's public house. He could see the police approaching the closed doors, the sudden revolver-fire from the barricaded windows— and machine-gun fire.

He did not need telling that Dragoli and his men were making a desperate effort to keep the police at bay while they made their escape through an unknown exit. That part of the East End was a regular rabbit-warren of alleys, little-known passages, short cuts to the river and the main road. More than likely there was an underground chamber at the Red Lion, like that of the Steam Packet's, where the dope had been stored.

The Toff swung the police car round a

corner and it lurched violently as the near-side wheels bumped upon the pavement and then sped over the uneven cobbles of the narrow road. Warrender grunted but knew that the Toff had complete control of the car. And speed was vital.

The car swerved again—into a second, longer turning. The road was empty and the Toff looked at the Assistant Commissioner.

'We're getting near,' he said. 'And I've an idea how to break through the barricade. It'll mean smashing the car up.

Warrender looked at lips which were set very tight and eyes which were like agate.

The Assistant Commissioner knew what the Toff meant and was silent for a moment. Then he nodded.

'Do what you like,' he said.

'Thanks! You'd better climb into the back seat, Sir Ian,' the Toff said quietly.

'I'll stay with you,' returned the Assistant Commissioner.

The Toff let it go at that. One more turning and they would see the Red Lion in front of them.

As the car swerved round the corner the Toff saw three police cars drawn up on the opposite side of the road to the Red Lion which was built on a corner site with a cobble parking-place in front of it and a drive for cars.

Farther up the road was an ambulance. At one spot a little crowd of men bent over a prostrate form on the ground. Dotted along the pavement opposite the pub were a dozen or more detectives, all crouching behind the cover of their cars.

An occasional bark of a revolver-shot coughed through the air on top of a little yellow stab of flame. And as the car drew nearer the scene the Toff saw a policeman's helmet lying in the courtyard—obviously belonging to one of the men who had been shot when McNab had started the raid.

The Toff was less than twenty yards away and in a few seconds he would succeed—or fail. Failure would be too fearful to contemplate.

They reached the first of the police cars lined up opposite the Red Lion. A man stood up, waving his arms wildly, and the Toff recognised McNab.

Warrender shouted something but McNab probably never heard it. He was dumbfounded at the Toff's sudden manoeuvre.

For as the big car reached the drive leading to the courtyard the Toff swung the wheel round fiercely. The car slithered round, tyres squealing, brakes grating as the Toff applied them to prevent the car from overturning. Then, crouching slightly forward with his eyes glinting like steel, the Toff set the front wheels towards the big saloon doors of the Red Lion.

From a window above came the bark of shots and from the rear of the police car a detective gasped as a bullet seared like a red-hot dagger through his shoulder. Another pierced the sleeve of the Toff's coat but his lips were curved in a mad dare-devilry and Warrender, next to him, gripped the sides of the car, waiting for the smash.

Then it came!

The nose of the car loomed up against the barricaded doors, then crashed into them. Wood splintered and groaned under the impact. The radiator of the car crumpled, the engine spluttered, coughed and went still as the car lurched sickeningly on one side.

Would it turn over?

For a horrible second the Toff thought that it would. He wrenched at the wheel, putting his whole weight behind the effort. Slowly, like a giant tortoise, the car righted itself.

Its nose was through the barricade! The door of the Red Lion swung open and the Toff caught a glimpse of the bottles and glasses on the shelves behind the bar.

The Toff jumped from his seat. He grabbed his gun from his pocket, spared a split-second for a glance at Warrender, who was pulling himself together from the force of the smash, and then tensed his muscles as he swung open the car door and jumped to the ground.

A bullet hummed past his ears, fired from somewhere inside the pub. The Toff took no notice. He vaulted over the radiator of the wrecked car and stood for a second in the doorway. Behind him Warrender and the uninjured detective were climbing through the opening.

The Toff pointed behind the bar and shouted over his shoulder.

'You can get to the stairs through that door,' he told the others. 'Once the front rooms are cleared of the brutes, McNab's men can get across.'

Then the Toff streaked across the saloon bar towards a second door, opening, he knew, into the rear quarters of the Red Lion. The door was shut but on the other side he heard the mutter of voices—Harry the Pug's among them.

The Toff put his gun to the lock of the door and a yellow stab of flame spat out. The bullet smashed through the lock and the door swung inwards. As he ducked and swerved, avoiding the rattle of bullets which swept through the open door, he saw Harry the Pug and one of Garrotty's thugs glaring towards him, smoking guns in their hands.

The Toff was taking no chances. Both crooks were in full view but he was hidden by the framework of the door. His hand jutted out and his gun spoke. Once—twice.

Harry the Pug dropped his gun and clapped his hands to his stomach. He staggered about, writhing, groaning. The second man just dropped in his tracks, a huddled heap on the bare floor.

The Toff stepped into the room. He slipped his gun in his pocket and caught the Pug's thick neck in his wiry fingers.

'Where's the girl?' he demanded and his voice was like a lash.

The Pug gurgled in his throat. There was no fight left in him. His only sensation was a terrible agony in his stomach and a fearful dread of the steel-eyed man who was glaring into his face. He choked. His right hand wavered towards a second door, opposite that through which the Toff had come.

'In—the—cellar . . .' gasped the Pug.

The Toff let him go and turned towards the door. It was shut but when he touched the handle he knew that it was not locked. He flung it open and darted behind the cover of the wall but nothing happened.

Then he looked through the opening and saw a flight of wooden steps, illuminated only by a single electric lamp jutting out of the wall at the bottom. Beyond it was an open door.

The Toff took out his gun again and stepped into the open. Still no sound came beyond the distant pattering of footsteps. The Toff dropped down the stairs, three at a time.

Was Anne Farraway all right?

His silent question was answered more quickly than he expected. As he went through the open door he saw a big, concrete-walled cellar, bare of everything but a line of cupboards running alongside one wall. The doors of the cupboards were open and with one exception they were empty. But in the last receptacle were stored countless little packages, all neatly sealed—just like the package which McNab had shown him at Scotland Yard. There was no doubt now as to where Dragoli had kept the dope.

But the Toff was thinking mostly of the girl. And he saw her, lying full length on the concrete floor in a far corner.

He rushed to her side and bent over her. A gag was tied tightly round her mouth, biting into the skin, but he cut through it quickly with his penknife.

There was a twist at the corners of his mouth.

'Here we are again, Annabelle. You all right?'

Anne Farraway nodded. She tried to speak but her voice was inaudible. For the first time the Toff saw that her arms and legs were bound.

'Keep still,' he said quietly and pulled a small flask of whisky from his hip pocket, forcing a trickle of the spirit down her parched throat. Then he cut through the rope which bound her and lifted her to a sitting position, supporting her with his firm arm.

He smiled.

'Everything's set, Annabelle. The police will be here in two shakes. Tell me'—his voice took on an urgency which it was impossible to repress—'do you know where Dragoli's gone? Which way?'

Anne spoke at last in a hoarse whisper.

'There's a switch,' she managed, 'beneath the electric-light switch over there. When you turn it a part of the wall opens and you can get through. Dragoli and Garrotty went five minutes ago—'

'Good girl!' breathed the Toff. 'Anything else?'

Anne forced herself to speak.

'They took a lot of that—stuff'—she pointed towards the empty cupboards and the one which still contained a small fortune's worth of cocaine—'with them. I think you can get through the passage to a house somewhere—and they've been loading the stuff into a removal van. I heard Dragoli telling Garrotty—'

'Annabelle,' breathed the Toff, 'you're a marvel! I'll see you later.'

He moved across to the electric switch and found the second control just as Anne had told him. A sound on the top of the stairs made him look up. McNab was there, hurrying down.

'You all right?' shouted the Chief Inspector.

'Right as two pins,' said the Toff, operating the switch. 'Send a man back, McNab. Dragoli's got a removal van outside a house in one of the side streets. You ought to get them—'

But someone called out above-stairs; McNab stopped swearing and he yelled:

'Upstairs—up fast, Rolleeson!'

The jubilation that the Toff was feeling because of the triumph of the forced entry disappeared. Rollison jumped towards Anne Farraway, lifted her off her feet and raced for the stairs. McNab turned and clumped up before them, blowing like a grampus.

The Toff had never experienced a worse moment of fear: it was the unknown menace, the cause of McNab's warning, that did the harm. He leapt from the top of the stairs as he reached the saloon. In front of him, but crowding back to the door, were a dozen men, police, Garrotty's gangsters. Warrender

Then the explosion came from behind him. He heard it, a terrific roar that seemed to shatter his eardrums and a gust of wind that lifted him clean off his feet. He was vaguely conscious of that dreadful roaring in his ears, of the girl flying from his grasp, of something that seemed to grip him like a giant's hand and tear at his limbs. And then for the second time that day blackness came over him.

Dragoli had covered his retreat by blowing the place up.

CHAPTER NINE

Forced Rest

Not one of the dozen-odd men who had been standing near the entrance to the cellar kept their feet. The force of the explosion sent them crashing and the people in the street heard the roar, saw the windows smashing outwards and the smoke billowing from the back of the Red Lion. An emergency squad of police rushed forward and started the work of rescue.

Those near the doors had escaped lightly. Warrender was conscious and scrambled to his feet. He saw the outstretched bodies about him, saw splashes of blood in a dozen places and his heart went heavy.

McNab, with the side of his head badly battered, was unconscious between Rollison and the door. The Toff was in a crumpled heap, with hardly a stitch of clothes left on him. His right arm was bleeding from a cut that ran from elbow to wrist.

Oddly enough, the girl had hardly suffered.

In Rollison's arms she had missed the full force of the blast of the explosion, sheltered by Rollison's body. She was dazed and frightened as she sat up but even her fall had been broken by the body of a man in the doorway. Her frock was black and torn but she looked presentable.

She did not recognise the grey-haired Warrender.

'Are you all right, Miss Farraway?'

'Yes—yes, I'm all right. But Mr Rollison—'

'He'll be well looked after,' muttered Warrender. He hated to pass on the fear in his mind—a dread that the Toff was dead with McNab. 'Get outside, please—'

Anne had seen Rollison's crumpled body and she hurried towards him. From below-stairs there was an ominous roaring and she was conscious again of a dreadful oppression and a heat that made breathing difficult. And then, as someone pushed past her and dragged Rollison upright, she saw a tongue of flame shoot up the stairs.

Below, the Red Lion was an inferno.

Yet she stuck it with the police and ambulance men who were getting the wounded on to stretchers. She felt cool and calm and the fact surprised her: perhaps it was because of her acquaintance with the Toff. Had he been conscious and active she could have imagined his easy smile, the gleam in his eyes as he encouraged the others to fiercer efforts.

As it was, it was a grim business.

Warrender took his coat off and worked as hard as any while the flames took a greater hold and smoke billowed into the wrecked saloon of the Red Lion. The heat was growing unbearable. Anne pushed her hair back from her eyes and her hand came away wet with sweat. Only three people, Rollison among them, were still inside.

Wind from the streets, coming easily through the smashed door, was nursing the flames. The walls at the head of the stairs were blazing, flames were licking along the counters.

Two policemen lifted Rollison gently, laying him on a stretcher. He was the last man to be carried out. Only Warrender and two others remained with the girl. The Assistant Commissioner's voice was gentle.

'Good work, Miss Farraway, we'll all remember it. Now outside, quickly.'

Anne went out. The coolness of the street air was refreshing yet did little to ease her burning forehead. The sightseers, pushed well away from the doomed building and the warehouses next to it that would be bound to suffer, were staring and muttering. From somewhere out of sight came the strident ringing of a fire-engine bell.

'Along here.' A detective-sergeant, detailed to look after the girl, took her arm. Dazedly she walked along a small alley at the back of the Red Lion. The police were in sole possession here for it was a cul-de-sac and a cordon of uniformed men prevented the crowd from pushing along it.

It was like an emergency field-dressing station.

Two doctors were working, although Anne did not realise who they were. Three ambulances were there, being loaded, and a lorry was used as an emergency couch for first aid.

All this—because the Toff had almost caught Dragoli.

Almost . . .

The girl felt cold, frightened. She had known Dragoli perhaps more than anyone else present. His wicked eyes, his cruelty, the devilishness of the man when he had tried to force her to speak—all those things came back to her slowly. Garrotty too. As far as she could tell, both the men had escaped.

The fight was not over; it had hardly started.

The police, thanks in the main to the Toff, had found one of the hide-outs of the Black Circle's organisation, had even succeeded in finding some of the stores. But the surprise had been prevented. The furniture van, loaded with cocaine, had escaped through the back streets, approached by a secret entrance from the Red Lion.

She knew, although no one had told her, that the van had escaped. Warrender would not have looked so grim but for that. The detective-sergeant, a cheerful young man named Owen, had told her who Warrender was. Owen was worried by the anxiety in the

103

girl's troubled eyes; and the fright.

'It'll be all right,' he assured her. 'A matter of time, that's all.'

'Is it?' she asked the question slowly. 'I—I don't know. If Mr Rollison is dead . . .'

Detective-Sergeant James Owen stared then shook his head and grinned.

'The Toff's not dead,' he said. 'He'll go on for ever.'

It was absurd, of course, and she knew it: yet the confidence with which the man spoke cheered her. If a policeman could really believe that the Toff was indestructible . . .

A path had been cleared now for the fire-engines and the brass helmets of the brigade that had arrived first glittered all about them. With smooth, almost clockwork precision, the escapes were run up, the hoses unfolded, water began to stream on to the burning buildings.

Smoke, flame and water and then steam, added to the magnificence of the spectacle and the roar of the fire. Owen pursed his lips and then shrugged.

'Three or four buildings'll go; we can't avoid it. Cigarette?'

'Thanks,' said Anne. She did not smoke a great deal but one then was a godsend. As she drew on it Sir Ian Warrender turned from one of the ambulances. His grey hair was streaked about his head and covered with grime, soot was daubed on his face and his clothes were filthy.

'We'll be able to get away now,' he said wearily.

'Mr—Rollison?'

'I think he'll pull through,' said Warrender.

But he did not seem confident and Anne Farraway hated the expression in his eyes. She said nothing as he led the way to a police car that had been brought into the cul-de-sac and he opened the door for her. The ambulances first threaded their way between the fire-engines and the police. Farther along the road cordons of police were forcing the surging crowds back. A thousand eyes were staring at the girl sitting next to Warrender.

Anne hardly noticed them.

She was remembering Dragoli and the things he had done. The murder of her brother. The dreadful affair near the London-Chelmsford road. The ordeal at the Steam Packet and the way the Toff had come, debonair, smiling, cheerful and single-handed—and damnably dangerous to Dragoli.

She believed the Toff could beat Dragoli but she was afraid of what would happen if he did not live to fight—or if he was forced to stand by indefinitely. The picture of his blood-stained face, the jagged wound in his arm, seemed to frighten her.

But what was worse was the conviction that only the Toff could beat Dragoli.

Without him . . . ?

The Black Circle would flourish: its influence, and the effect of the drug it was distributing, would grow. And she knew that while she was alive Dragoli would watch and wait for her. Indirectly she had caused the smashing of the Red Lion, the loss of thousands of pounds' worth of the drug.

She shivered, because she felt afraid.

*   *   *

It was just twenty-four hours after the affair at the Red Lion, Shadwell, that a clean-shaven, yellow-faced man with narrow, compelling eyes looked up from the evening paper he was reading into the glittering eyes of a tough-faced man sitting by a table with one ugly hand on the neck of a whisky bottle.

The room was well-furnished, although it was badly littered. No one seemed to have worried whether anything unwanted went on the floor, the tables, the chairs or the cupboards. Three daily papers were lying about the room, one of them ripped across. There were two empty whisky bottles on the floor and a broken glass.

Few people would have recognised the clean-shaven man as Achmed Dragoli until he spoke. His voice was as slow and measured as ever and anyone who had known him well would have seen in their mind's eye the long, silky beard, the heavy eyebrows.

'You're drinking too much, Garrotty.'

'Aw, shucks!' The American lifted the bottle without troubling to use a glass and emptied some of its fiery contents down his capacious throat. He drank neat whisky like water. 'We gotta live, Drag.'

'Ye-es.' Dragoli spoke very softly. 'We've got to live, a long time, and there is a great deal of work to do. It's to be done—sober.'

He leaned forward and snatched the bottle. It clattered from Garrotty's grasp to the floor, crashed, and the whisky spilled out. Garrotty's face flushed an ugly red and his hand darted towards his shoulder-holster.

But Dragoli had a gun in his hand before the half-tipsy gangster could draw.

Garrotty's eyes narrowed venomously but his hand moved away and his lips formed a grudging apology.

'OK, Drag. No need for that between friends.'

'I'm glad you think so,' said Dragoli but he kept his gun in sight. 'Listen, you fool. We have six months or more to go, most of the cocaine to be unloaded and—a quarter of a million pounds to collect. Does that make sense?'

Garrotty stared. The figure mentioned was seeping through the whisky fumes that had befuddled his brain.

'How—hic—how much wassat?'

'A quarter of a million.'

107

'P-pounds or dollars?'

'English pounds,' said Dragoli slowly. 'And your share could be a big one. Say a quarter. Will that make you change your mind and stop drinking? You've taken enough since last night to last most men a year.'

Garrotty grinned, a little sheepishly. He lifted his hands and dropped them. Cupidity, not hate, was glittering in his eyes and he wiped his shirt-sleeve across his wet lips.

'Jus' a little holiday, Drag; yuh can't say no t' thet.'

Dragoli shrugged.

'Don't have too many of them. We are safe enough here and five of your friends are able to work. In addition,' he added slowly, 'to the rest of my own friends, ready to work in England. But we shall do most of the actual handling of the cocaine, Garrotty. Understand?'

'Sure—sure. I understand.' Garrotty wiped his lips again and staggered up from the table. He went to the window and pushed it up, although it was pitch dark outside.

Silence greeted him.

The silence of the countryside after dark, broken by the odd murmurings of the trees and hedges and the night birds and yet intensified by it. The cool air did him good. He turned round, cumbersomely, and he no longer looked drunk.

'All right, Dragoli. I'm with you. But there's

one thing I'm worried about. The Toff . . .'

He spoke casually but he failed to make the words seem casual. In that room, on the top floor of a small country house near Camberley, in Surrey, the presence of the Toff seemed to make itself felt, although he was thirty miles away and helpless in a hospital. Garrotty, for the first time, was really beginning to feel the influence of the Toff.

So was Dragoli but he succeeded in hiding his fear.

'He's finished for weeks, Garrotty, if not for longer. Don't worry about him.'

'I don't trust de guy,' said Garrotty. 'Dere's just one way I'd like to see the Toff and that's in a box. Sure.' He scowled and lit a cigarette, letting it droop from the corner of his thick lips. 'In a box, Dragoli, an' I reckon I'd pay somep'n to put him there myself.'

'You'll have the chance,' said Dragoli. 'But we will forget the Toff while he is in hospital. According to this'—he lifted the evening paper—'he is in a bad way. An emergency operation was performed this morning.'

Garrotty grinned.

'That so? Good hearing, Drag. How many of the dicks got theirs?'

'One more died, in hospital' said Dragoli. 'Three were dead last night. Harry's dead too.'

'That won't make me keep awake at nights,' sneered Garrotty. 'The squirt was scared all through.'

Dragoli laughed, showing his yellow teeth.

'Of the Toff,' he said. 'But remember this. We have made it impossible to work in the open much now. The police are different over here from what they are in your country and they won't take kindly to the death of three detectives.'

There was a swagger in Garrotty's manner as he went towards a radiogram in a corner of the big room.

'That so? They ain't so dumb in Noo York State, Mister, an' I reckon I saw the way to get past 'em. I'm not worryin'.'

'Excellent,' said Dragoli smoothly. 'Well, our next big task, Garrotty, is Colliss.'

Garrotty swung round from the radio.

'Dat guy, huh! What's on him?'

'A great deal. Colliss is home from Stamboul, as I told you before—last night's interruption. He had been investigating the Black Circle for the police over there and he is to contact with Scotland Yard. He is first, of course, going to his country house. It is believed that he visited Turkey solely as an archaeologist. The English police are showing some imagination, my friend, for they are realising the importance of the Black Circle.' He laughed, as though at some secret joke. 'But there are leakages of information at Scotland Yard—'

'Sure, graft,' grunted Garrotty. 'You can't tell a Noo Yorker about dat, Drag.'

'It is more difficult in England,' said Dragoli. 'The information came somewhat reluctantly and the price paid was considerable. But this afternoon I had information that Colliss can give the police some unpleasant facts. Facts that might prevent us from earning that large sum of money.'

Garrotty's eyes glittered.

'Where's de guy?'

Dragoli laughed, well satisfied.

'That is what I wanted to hear. Colliss, as it happens, lives near Winchester. On this road. I want you to take two of your men and rub him out. Here is a photograph.'

Dragoli took a wallet from his pocket, slipped a postcard photograph from it and handed it to Garrotty. The gangster stared at the photograph of a thick-set man whose large mouth and chin seemed out of proportion to the rest of his face.

'I got him.' Garrotty passed the photograph back. 'I'll put him out for ten an' more, Boss. When do I start?'

'The police are visiting him the day after tomorrow, at ten o'clock in the morning. Tomorrow night is the best opportunity, Garrotty.'

'OK. I'll fix it.' Garrotty grinned, wiped his forehead with a dirty handkerchief and at last switched on the radio. It was just after nine o'clock and he scowled when he heard the end of the weather report.

'Keep it there!' Dragoli snapped as the gangster was about to turn the dial to a more amusing subject. Garrotty scowled but obeyed. The measured voice of the BBC announcer came over the wires and Garrotty's hands tightened while Dragoli let the paper fall from his grasp.

'We regret to announce,' said the radio dispassionately, 'yet another death as a result of last night's East End explosion following a battle between police and gangsters. At half past seven this evening the Hon Richard Rollison succumbed to his wounds. The revelation of his great part in the fight against crime was a surprise to his many friends in London. Mr Rollison was born in nineteen . . .'

Dragoli and Garrotty heard nothing more. They stared at each other, expressionlessly at first; then Garrotty began to laugh.

The laugh echoed about the room and sounded far worse when Dragoli joined in.

CHAPTER TEN

Mr. Reginald Colliss

The Toff, in a sitting position and with bandages round his head and his right arm strapped to his side, managed to put something of his old insouciance into his expression, something of the old devil-may-care gleam in his one visible eye.

'Miss Farraway,' he said with mock ferocity, 'you're proving a nuisance and a worry. There are supposed to be only five people concerned in the conspiracy to make me die and you are not included.'

Anne laughed, softly.

'I hope you're not really annoyed. I can't see you properly with those bandages on.'

'Oh, save me!' appealed the Toff; lifting his left arm towards the white ceiling of the small private ward in the nursing-home to which he had been shifted from the Grandley Hospital only three hours before. 'You've known me about five minutes, and after your job with Dragoli and Garrotty you ought to be beyond lifting your voice above a whisper, and here you are trying to humour me.' He paused. 'Hand me a cigarette, Anne, and you'd better light it for me. Then, as you've worried Warrender's life out until he let you come, I'll tell you. Don't say that I haven't warned you that I've a tortuous mind.'

'I don't mind what kind of mind you've got, providing you're alive,' said Anne. She lit a cigarette, took it from her lips and pushed it between his. Rollison made a scowl with the visible half of his face.

'If your husband-to-be could see you doing that he would probably sue me for divorce or breach of promise. I can—'

113

'You mean *I* can manage my husband-to-be,' said Anne, 'and after all he can't very well grumble at me lighting a cigarette for a corpse.' Her eyes were gleaming and Rollison leaned back in his pillows, puffing contentedly and studying her.

It was easy to understand now how she had managed to hold out against the pressure of Dragoli's gang. She had great spirit, a deep understanding. He knew that he was already fond of her and he hoped that he did not for once let his heart rule his head. But she was young: no more than twenty-two or three. That made her complete self-possession the more remarkable.

It was the morning after the radio and newspaper announcements of his death. It had taken him several hours and a great deal of effort to get the announcement put out. No one, not even Warrender, had liked the idea of it. But Warrender had learned a great deal since the affair at the Red Lion and he knew just how impressive was the Toff's reputation in the East End. From Harry the Pug, before he had died, Squinty and others, he had discovered the not very palatable fact that the Toff was more feared by the gentlemen of crime than were the police.

Apparently Rollison had been unconscious all the way from the Red Lion to the hospital. There he had gathered strength enough to ask for Warrender. The Assistant Commissioner

114

and a doctor had been present when the Toff's one eye had opened to its widest and his lips had curved in a cheerful smile.

'I'm a lot better now the crowd's away.'

To say the least of it, the startling recovery had been a surprise. Before Warrender and the house-surgeon had been able to make any intelligent comment the Toff had explained that although he had had a nasty packet he had not lost consciousness but he had considered it an excellent idea to play possum. His idea broadened. Many people including, in all likelihood, many of Dragoli's people, had seen him looking badly wounded. It would be an excellent idea if he died, from two points of view.

First, he said firmly, Dragoli and Garrotty and any others concerned in the menacing association of the Black Circle would be inclined to take more chances. He said, as gently as possible, that he believed they would be more scared of the Toff than of the police and in the light of his recent discoveries Warrender had been forced to admit that was true.

'Right,' the Toff had said. 'Point one: with the Black Circle operatives in this country a little careless, when I'm in fighting order again I can manage to pull something off against them. When I virtually rise from the dead I can promise you that a lot of people of the Harry-the-Pug kidney are going to be a damned sight more careful of me in future. You may not be inclined to believe it but as the Toff I have a strong corrective influence on all manner of queer people.'

Warrender had admitted that was probably true; and later, reluctantly, had agreed to let it be reported that Rollison was dead.

After the announcement he had been smuggled from the hospital to a private nursing-home only a few hundred yards from his Gresham Terrace flat. Warrender, a nurse, the surgeon, Jolly and Chief Inspector McNab—also wounded—had been the only people concerned in the trick. Warrender covered the house-surgeon and the nurse against any possible trouble for making out false death certificates: and officially, at half past seven on the previous evening, the Toff had died.

Anne Farraway had been told by Warrender. Just why she had disbelieved it she hardly knew. Perhaps it was the fact that the Assistant Commissioner did not look as worried and grieved as he should have been.

Showing something of the persistence with which she had refused to answer Garrotty's questions, she had pestered Warrender, stating frankly that she thought it was false. Finally, and because Warrender was afraid she would start making unnecessary investigations, he had told Rollison.

Now the girl was sitting by the side of the

Toff's bed and smiling somewhat whimsically. The man who married her, thought the Toff, was going to be lucky and God help him if he didn't deserve her.

'And there you are,' he said after five minutes of brisk talking. 'Now I'm tired and the nurse will tell you shortly that I'm ill. My name, remember, is not Rollison but Browning. Mr Bernard Browning, as a matter of fact, and I hope to be up and doing in a couple of weeks.'

Anne nodded. She guessed that the wounded arm—he had jagged it along a broken bottle when he had fallen and another broken piece of glass had been responsible for the cut over his left eye—was worse than he made out, otherwise he would not have been prepared to wait for a fortnight.

'That's fine. But—what happens meanwhile?'

'I wish I knew,' said the Toff and he closed his eye. He looked weary and worried and the nurse frowned when she entered a few seconds afterwards. Anne stood up but the Toff stopped her with a raised hand.

'Listen, young lady. This fiancé of yours: where is he?'

'At Wisford Hotel. I sent for him—'

'And of course he came running. Has he got a family?'

She looked puzzled.

'No, he lives in lodgings at the moment.

Why?'

'Just this,' said Rollison slowly. 'I wouldn't put it past Dragoli to try and get his own back and I don't want you to get in the front line. What's his name, by the way?'

'Frensham—Ted Frensham.'

'Well, he sounds all right,' admitted the Toff dubiously. 'I hope he is because I'm going to suggest that you stay with some friends of mine. Excellent people but in Surrey and not in Essex.'

'I could stay here and help to look after you,' suggested Anne Farraway.

'You could not,' said the Toff. 'In the first place, I'm an impressionable man and in the second I don't want to break your heart or the heart of Mr Frensham. Will you go?'

The girl hesitated.

'Who—who are these people?'

'Named Tennant. Bob and Patricia. They're quite respectable, they've a nice house and servants to look after them. I know it means giving up your job but there's a lot to be said for sliding out of Dragoli's reach. And if he should happen to find you, I can't think of a better man than Bob Tennant—barring myself, of course,' he added with a smile that seemed a little tired, 'to take care of you. I've asked them to meet you at the Eclat Hotel for lunch, anyhow, so—'

The nurse stirred impatiently. Anne Farraway stood up quickly, pressed the Toff's left hand, thanked him and promised she would take no chances. The Toff laid back wearily after she had gone and he was asleep before he started thinking seriously of what he would do when he was on his feet again.

* * *

Chief-Inspector McNab, heavily bandaged and groaning when he moved in his bed, eyed the Assistant Commissioner glumly. 'I wish I could get to see Colliss, sir, but—'

'Don't talk nonsense,' said Warrender with a smile. 'I'll go down and see him myself, McNab. According to his report he knows something we can bite on but he says he does not think there is any desperate hurry. This Black Circle thing has not been working too long. We found it in good time.'

'I'm hoping so,' said McNab who would never have scored high marks for optimism.

Warrender laughed more lightly than he felt and left the ward.

He thought of the Toff as he stepped into a taxi, after ordering the driver to take him to Scotland Yard. It was right enough up to a point but he wished he had been more careful about allowing it to be told 'officially' that the Hon Richard Rollison was dead.

But Rollison on his feet could look after himself while one thing was certain: while he was in the private nursing-home no one from

119

Dragoli's Black Circle would discover that he was alive and he would have a better chance of recovering.

An evening paper on his desk when he reached the office towards nine o'clock—he was up early during the Black Circle schemozzle—still carried headlines about the outrage in Shadwell. There had been a great stir in the Yard and farther along in Whitehall. The Home Secretary himself had shown interest and concern but Warrender had not yet felt justified in raising a real scare.

No one more than Warrender could appreciate the damnable effect of a widespread habit of taking cocaine.

It was practised, of course, among a small circle of erotic wastrels in every big town. Probably three or four thousand people in London were victims. But from the amount of dope that had been seen by McNab and Rollison at the Red Lion and destroyed in the fire, there were supplies enough to last London's normal clientele for years.

It would not be the first time that efforts had been made to make the drug habit more widespread. Its effect was more insidious than anything else and Warrender, with good reason, considered it the biggest crime. Now it was being practised on a big scale and he did not want to cause an alarm.

The fact that Garrotty had been employed by Dragoli had helped him.

The official police story was that Garrotty was making an attempt to start gang-warfare in London. That had satisfied the demands of the Press and to a point it was true. There had been a great commotion on the placards and in the newspapers on the morning following the raid and Scotland Yard had been warmly congratulated on its great effort to wipe out the threat of gangsterdom.

Warrender's lips twisted.

Without the Toff the raid would never have taken place. Had he been told, without being shown evidence, he would have doubted the possibility of one man being able to do what Rollison had done. But there it was . . .

Warrender looked at his watch and pressed a bell for a sergeant. It was fair-haired Detective-Sergeant Owen and Warrender smiled a little.

'Owen, we're going into the country for a breath of air.'

The Assistant Commissioner was popular with the CID officials because he was not above joking mildly with them, in direct contrast to the efforts of the other ACs. 'Have a fast car and be outside at nine-thirty, will you?'

'Yes, sir.' Owen, curly haired and cheerful to look at, left the office with satisfaction. A day virtually off duty was a rare thing.

Warrender telephoned to Mr Reginald Colliss, the well-known archaeologist who was not so well known as a special agent of the Yard, and told him that McNab would not be able to get along the following morning and that he, Warrender, had determined to go along instead.

'It's a day earlier,' he said, 'but it's urgent, Colliss.'

'I'll be in,' promised Reginald Colliss.

*   *   *

When he had finished talking to the Assistant Commissioner, Colliss leaned back thoughtfully in his chair. As the photograph that Garrotty had seen had emphasised, he had a very full jaw and very full lips. Yet, oddly enough, when in repose he looked handsome, perhaps because of his well-shaped nose and the pair of fine grey eyes that gazed at all and sundry with a cool, detached air that hid most of his thoughts.

In many ways Colliss was worried.

He stood up and walked towards the window. The sun was shining, the green lawn looked cool and refreshing. After the heat and sweat of Stamboul, England was a paradise.

He was above medium height and his shoulders were very thick. Yet his hands and feet were smaller than the average, the hands white and carefully tended. His hair was rather long and crisp and when he smiled little lines crept into the corners of his eyes.

The wrinkles appeared suddenly but he was not smiling.

He had seen the movement in the shrubbery at the end of the lawn. It was not the wind and he did not believe that it was a cat or dog, or even a rabbit. There was something darker there than there should have been.

He drew towards the wall a little, his eyes narrowed.

The dark thing moved. He could just make out the figure of a man slipping through the shrubbery to the side of the lawn. The man was lost from sight in a small thicket.

Colliss pursed his lips as he turned towards his desk.

He opened the top drawer and took out a heavy Army revolver. It was fully loaded and, despite his small hands, he carried it lightly and purposefully back to the window.

There was the slightest rustle of sound outside.

Colliss moved quickly to try and catch a glimpse of whoever was near but he failed. For from the far edge of the lawn he saw another figure, a squat, swarthy man, crouching low and pointing something towards the house.

The shot came a split second later.

Colliss jumped to one side. The glass of the window smashed into a thousand pieces, one splinter sticking into the special agent's coat. Colliss returned the fire but several shots were coming and he knew that he had more than two men to deal with.

Then a gun appeared close to the window.

Colliss could not see the man carrying it. Just the gun and the hand that held it showed. He had not time to move out of the line of fire; he raised his own gun.

The two shots echoed simultaneously and Colliss's gun fell from his hand.

CHAPTER ELEVEN

Dragoli Is Annoyed

Garrotty stood in the french windows of Colliss's Winchester house. His automatic was smoking. There was blood on Colliss's fingers and the man on the floor looked unconscious. Garrotty moved quickly across the room while footsteps and cries of alarm came from the other side.

His lips twisted, he flung the door open.

Two women and two men stood in the passage. They had been running and each one stopped at the sight of Garrotty and the gun. Fear beyond all reason showed on their faces as the gangster, forbidding and menacing, lifted the automatic a little. A red-faced maid screeched.

Garrotty's thick voice flung a question. Over his mouth and chin he was wearing a handkerchief, over his eyes the brim of a wide-brimmed hat was pulled well down.

'How many more in de house—you?'

He stabbed his gun towards the first man, plump, middle-aged and dressed in black—Colliss's butler for twenty-five years. The man gasped the words out:

'None, we're all here, we—'

'Turn around,' snapped Garrotty.

The butler was the only one to hesitate and Garrotty loosed a shot towards the man's feet. It worked; the butler swung round. Another swarthy-faced man joined Garrotty, masked as he was, and Garrotty nodded. The second gangster used a black jack with equal force on men and women. Four people dropped, quite unconscious, to the floor of the passage.

'Find a room wit' a small window and push dem in,' snapped Garrotty. 'Move fast, Red, we ain't losin' no time.'

The man named Red said nothing but hurried along the passage while Garrotty turned back to the room where Colliss was lying. A third gangster was standing by the window, watching the grounds, although there was little chance of an interruption.

Colliss's house was built well away from the main road. The archaeologist had always had a passion for the country and he had buried himself on this little five-acre patch of grass and woodland with a ten-roomed house that was amply large enough for his bachelor requirements. The nearest building, according to Dragoli's report when he had given the gangster particulars of the place, was a mile and a half away. Anyone who might have heard the shooting at a mile and a half would have taken it for granted that it came from an ordinary morning shoot for birds or rabbits.

'Fasten his legs,' Garrotty snapped.

The third gangster obeyed, using thin tough cord, while Garrotty started to go through the contents of the study. Bureaux, drawers and cupboards were smashed open and the papers taken out. In five minutes Garrotty had every available paper on the desk by a wall and at the same moment Colliss stirred, groaning a little. Garrotty swung towards him and fear showed in the special agent's eyes as the gun moved close to his head.

'Talk fast,' snarled Garrotty; he had learned almost from childhood how to strike fear in others and it came as a habit. 'Where's de dope on de Black Circle racket, Colliss?'

Colliss hesitated. Garrotty bent down and struck him brutally across the face. Colliss writhed in his bonds and the gangster hit him again. Colliss sobbed:

'In—in the safe! In—my—bedroom.'

'De keys?'

'In—my pocket,' Colliss gasped.

Garrotty bent down, tapped the man's body over expertly, found the keys and took them out. In five minutes he had located Colliss's bedroom, opened the safe and obtained the papers. They meant nothing to him but they would be what Dragoli wanted. Garrotty believed that he knew when a man had talked all he could and, as he entered the room, he snapped orders to his fellows; the gangster who had hit the servants had returned, after locking them in a pantry at the back of the house.

'OK,' grunted Garrotty, 'we're through. Get de car started, Red.'

Red, a fringe of red hair showing at the back of his head beneath his hat, stepped out on to the lawn. The second man followed him. Garrotty turned round, his lips twisted.

Colliss's eyes still showed his fear and Garrotty laughed harshly.

'You oughta learned how to take it, fella. So long.'

He lifted his gun a couple of inches and touched the trigger. Four shots rang out in quick succession hitting Colliss in the chest. Colliss leapt upwards convulsively and then crashed down.

Garrotty rubbed his fingers across his nose and stepped after the others. Three minutes later the noise of a car engine starting in the by-lane at the back of Colliss's house broke the silence of the countryside.

*   *   *

127

The house in Camberley where Achmed Dragoli was staying was like Colliss's place in many ways, although it was closer to the town and the main road. It had ten acres of its own grounds and it had been let furnished a month before to a man who called himself Smithers. Dragoli had several furnished houses about the country; he knew that there was the possibility of needing several hideouts in case of trouble and he was well prepared.

Garrotty was grinning complacently.

'I put him over, brodder, and I reckon you'll be interested in dese.' He dumped a case containing the papers from Colliss on a table. The room on the second floor of the house was in much better order now for Dragoli had obtained servants, all male, who could use a gun and cook a seven-course dinner with equal facility.

'De lot in de envelope,' said Garrotty with pride, 'come from de safe, Boss, an' Colliss reckoned dey was all 'bout de Black Circle.'

Dragoli nodded, without speaking, and took the papers out. There were a dozen, many of them no more than brief pencil sketches with a few notes scribbled on in ink. His expression did not alter as he looked through one thing after the other. Then:

'Where are the rest?'

'In de case,' said Garrotty with understandable surprise for Dragoli was standing nearer to them.

'Give me them.'

Garrotty, who for years had ruled one of the biggest rackets in New York City, had never known a man who could make him feel as scared as Dragoli did. He took out the papers, spreading them in front of the Egyptian. Dragoli went through them slowly, putting them all in a growing heap on the table. He did not speak until he had finished and then his baleful eyes looked murderous.

'You—helpless—fool!' he said very softly. 'There's nothing here—nothing at all.'

Garrotty gasped.

'But—but de guy—'

'Tricked you,' sneered Dragoli. 'Told you what he wanted you to believe and you let him do it. Do you know what these are, Garrotty?'

Garrotty's tongue ran along his dry lips.

'Say—'

'They are maps and plans of the location of Ancient Egyptian burial grounds near Cairo,' said Dragoli. 'Where you ought to be—'

'Say, listen—'

'Oh, get out of my sight!' snarled Dragoli.

Garrotty shrugged but went to the door. He was halfway out when Dragoli called after him:

'You're sure you killed Colliss?'

'Sure's I'm here.'

'All right,' said Dragoli and he took a cigarette from his case, lit it and sat down in an easy chair. The chief thing he had wanted to do was to have Colliss dead. It would have

129

been a help had he been able to find papers showing what the man had discovered when he had been in Stamboul but there was just a chance that he had committed them all to memory.

On the other hand, the fact that he had deceived Garrotty made it seem likely that the papers were in existence.

Dragoli smoked in silence for ten minutes then put the cigarette out and took a small rubber wallet from his pocket. It was filled with narrow slips of papers, like the contents of a Seidlitz-powder packet. He took one, opened it and tossed it down his throat. Then he closed his eyes and a soft, dreamy smile curved his full lips.

*   *   *

At a quarter past nine Sir Ian Warrender had finished talking with Colliss. At half-past nine Garrotty had fired those four shots at the special agent's heart. And at twenty-five minutes past eleven Sir Ian's car, driven by Detective Sergeant Owen, turned into the small drive of 'Holmlea,' Colliss's house.

There was no suggestion of trouble outside. Peace and silence reigned over the countryside and Owen drank in the clean air, telling himself that the day off duty was going to be fully up to his expectations.

It was Warrender, glancing from the drive

130

across the lawn, who saw the open french windows. He snapped an order at once.

'Pull up, Owen!'

The sergeant pulled at the brakes. Both men glanced across the lawn and Owen saw what Warrender had fancied at his first look. The french windows were smashed.

Warrender skipped out of the car with surprising agility for a man approaching sixty and Owen had a job to keep pace with him. As they drew nearer they saw the broken glass and, through the smashed panels, the sight of a man's leg, the toe pointing towards the ceiling.

Warrender was very pale.

'They've been here,' he said savagely. 'I hope to God we're in time. Draw your gun, Owen.'

Detective Sergeant Owen—who, because he was detailed to work on the Black Circle case, was carrying a .35 automatic—did as he was told. Cautiously they approached Colliss's study but no sound came. The sun, behind them, sent long shadows into the room as they stepped over the narrow gravel path. Then very softly came a voice, filled with uncertainty.

'Who is there?'

It was a whisper and Warrender knew that it was nothing to be alarmed about. He called out quickly:

'The police—'

'Thank God for that! Come in.'

Owen went in first, conscious of the possibility that it was a trick and that Warrender might be shot. He saw Colliss stretched out where Garrotty had left him for dead, bound hand and foot. Warrender followed and swore.

'Who—'

'Get me free,' gasped Colliss. 'And whisky—over there.'

*   *   *

So Colliss was not dead. Owen cut the cords and Warrender found and poured out the whisky. Colliss took a deep swallow and then pushed his hand through his hair. Owen had made him lean against the table and he was still sitting down. The blood on his hand and forehead had congealed into an unpleasant brown crust.

'Gunmen,' he said. 'Masked and I couldn't recognise them. If it hadn't been for your warnings, Sir Ian . . .'

Owen looked puzzled.

Warrender was on his knees, undoing the wounded man's waistcoat. To his astonishment, Owen saw something glitter beneath it; a mail-shirt. Round the heart were the marks of the four bullets which had lodged in his clothing.

'Find the servants,' begged Colliss and Owen jumped for the door at a nod from

Warrender. He left the door open but Colliss spoke quickly.

'It's all right—they got nothing.' He smiled faintly. 'They thought they'd put the fear of God into me and they damned nearly had. I didn't dream it was as bad as this, Sir Ian.'

Warrender's smile was tight-lipped.

'Nor do a lot of people. I won't take credit for suggesting the mail-shirt, though: Rollison told me it was essential and I even wear one myself.' He was smiling wryly, while the other man said:

'Rollison?'

'The Hon Richard Rollison.'

Colliss frowned, wiping his hand across his forehead.

'I know him, of course, but I thought—'

'That he was just an ornament,' smiled Warrender. 'A great many people do. Have you ever heard rumours of a man named the Toff?'

'I can't say I have,' admitted Colliss, making an effort to get up. 'Why?'

'That's Rollison's nickname in the East End; but you'll have plenty of time to learn about it. If you'd been much in England lately you'd know Rollison all right. How're you feeling?'

'Stiff and sore,' admitted Colliss. 'I had to fox, though, and if he'd fired at my head—'

He broke off.

Before Warrender spoke again he helped the man on to a couch and telephoned the

133

Winchester police. Meanwhile, Owen had found the servants, two of them still unconscious but none of them badly hurt. Morley, the butler, had recovered from the shock quickly and proved an expert in first aid. Bandaged and feeling comfortable, Colliss told the whole story. How he had seen the man in the grounds, been surprised by the others, shot and then—when Garrotty had finished with him—left for dead.

Warrender nodded slowly.

'You've a lot in common with Rollison,' he said. 'In fact you're the second man left for dead who's very much alive.'

'The Winchester people, sir.' Owen spoke from the doorway.

'Oh—send the Inspector in,' said Warrender.

He was annoyed that he had spoken of Rollison's ruse in Owen's hearing but he saw no reason for believing that the man would allow his knowledge to leak out. He made a mental note to warn Owen later and then concerned himself with orders to the local police against the possibility of further attempts on Colliss's life, three police to take up residence at the house until further orders.

The formalities finished, Warrender had a chance of learning what Colliss had discovered in Stamboul about the Black Circle.

What he learned did not make him happy.

CHAPTER TWELVE

Time Flies

In any other form of organised crime, nothing happening would have been a good omen. It would have suggested that the gentry concerned had been made nervous of further efforts and given the police time to make full inquiries.

When, for a week, nothing happened in the Dragoli case Warrender was, if anything, more gloomy than he had been when he had heard Colliss's report.

No reports were received that might have led to the finding of Dragoli, Garrotty or the other members of the gang. No discoveries of caches of 'snow' were reported. True, there was no suggestion that the use of cocaine was getting appreciably more widespread than it had for years but Warrender and others knew that was negligible evidence. It would take months, perhaps years, for the really malicious effect of the drug to materialise. A hundred thousand people might have been introduced to it in a week without the police getting an inkling of the truth.

Colliss had recovered quickly from his slight wounds and was still guarded at 'Holmlea.' Chief Inspector McNab carried his left arm in a sling but was on duty. Detective-Sergeant Owen was still attached to the case with another Chief Inspector, whose discretion was thoroughly dependable, by name Wilkinson. Others, without knowing the real importance of the affair, had been engaged in trying to trace Garrotty and Dragoli, without success.

With McNab, Warrender called at the nursing-home where the Hon Richard Rollison was still staying, some ten days after the explosion at Shadwell. Rollison was up, clad in a brilliant dressing-gown and sitting back with all his old assurance in an easy chair that normally had no place in the room's furnishing.

Rollison had a small table in front of him and a fountain-pen in his left hand. He grinned up as Warrender and McNab entered but went on with his job, the left hand moving slowly but firmly. Warrender frowned.

'Taking art lessons, Rollison?'

The Toff smiled and flipped a card across to the Assistant Commissioner, who managed to catch it.

'Making the left hand do what the right ought to,' he said lightly. 'All in the way of business, Sir Ian.'

Warrender frowned down at a little, carefully executed drawing. A top hat set at a rakish angle, a monocle and a cigarette-holder and the bow tie. It was the first time he had looked on one of the visiting-cards that had once scared the life out of the deceased Harry the Pug.

'My dear man—'

'You haven't heard me lecture,' said the Toff, finishing a sketch with a flourish and laying his pen down, 'on the merits of psychological terrorism and you've missed a treat. Hasn't he, Inspector? One of these cards, by the grace of God and a lot of luck, gets many folk worried. But that's by the way—how're things?'

'I don't like them,' admitted Warrender.

'Anything particular?' asked Rollison. His right arm was in a sling, to match McNab's left, but the bandages were off his head. Two pieces of sticking-plaster decorated his left cheek.

'Well, no. Except . . .'

He launched into a recital of what Colliss had told him.

Colliss had managed to get a great deal of information in Stamboul, although little of it was definite. He had identified Dragoli, however, as an agent of a cocaine ring in Stamboul. Arrangements had been made, and apparently were working smoothly, for the smuggling of the drug from China, across country to Stamboul and then into Europe. The Black Circle was a wide organisation— and the Stamboul authorities had been able to do little to stop its progress. It was a mixture, according to Colliss, of an Oriental Ku-Klux-

Klan and the OGPU. It had representatives in all manner of high places in Turkey and Egypt and there seemed little chance of intercepting the supply of cocaine at its source.

'Of course, we shall warn the other countries,' said Warrender. 'But our big task, Rollison, is to stop it getting a real hold in England.' Rollison grinned.

'A damned sight better to stop it at the source but I'll agree it's not going to be easy. I'd like to meet this man Colliss, though, he seems promising. I—come in.'

It was the nurse and Rollison gave a mock frown.

'Now, listen, I'm convalescing, Alice, and I won't be warned not to get excited. I never do, anyhow, and—'

'This has just come in, sir,' said the nurse, a middle-aged woman who had found it impossible to be severe with the Toff for long.

Rollison smiled as he took a letter, addressed to Mr Bernard Browning. It might have been from Jolly, at the flat, or from Anne Farraway—but he had had a note from Anne on the previous day, saying that she was enjoying her stay with the Tennants and that Ted Frensham, at her hosts' invitation, was spending a few days in Surrey.

Moreover, he did not recognise the writing on the envelope.

With a murmured apology, he tore it open. And then he stared down, his face very hard.

Warrender eyed him with growing alarm.

'What is it, man?'

Rollison's eyes held an expression that Warrender had never seen in them before.

'Just a friendly little note,' said the Toff bitterly. 'From Dragoli.'

A pin would have sounded like a tin kettle dropping in the room as Warrender and McNab eyed the speaker. Rollison handed them the letter. It was typewritten, although the envelope had been addressed in handwriting, and it said simply:

Clever, Rollison, but not clever enough.

Warrender pushed his hand through his hair.

'But—it's impossible!'

It's possible and it happened. How many people knew of this? Five . . .'

Warrender sat heavily on the bed.

'Seven. I told Colliss and Owen heard me.'

'Owen?'

'My sergeant,' explained McNab.

Rollison looked at both men without speaking then he stood up, taking a box of cigarettes from the table.

'Well, the scheme's busted and we can't undo it. I wish to heaven I could get busy.'

'Don't you realise,' said Warrender slowly, 'that someone must have told Dragoli about it? By the way, there's Miss Farraway, and she *might* have taken your friends into her confidence,'

'She might have done,' admitted the Toff 'but the Tennants are as reliable as I am. We'll assume she didn't. We'll assume that there are eight people altogether who knew the truth—and that's seven too many,' he added bitterly. 'Yourself, Colliss, McNab, Owen, the nurse here, the house-surgeon at Grandley's—and I don't think he would talk—Anne Farraway and my man Jolly, as well as the innocent victim of the conspiracy, myself. And one of us talked.'

Warrender looked pale.

'Dragoli—'

'Couldn't have guessed,' said the Toff and then suddenly he laughed. 'Well, we'll find out and it doesn't matter much.'

'Don't you think so? If there's a leakage of secret information like that—'

It might have been from the hospital,' Rollison said. 'Dragoli's too deep to be taken in by anything without checking up and when he learned that Colliss had put it across him he probably felt worried and started investigating. Forget it. I'm old enough to look after myself and I'm moving from here right away. I can rely on Jolly's cooking but I'm damned if I'd enjoy the food here after this.'

It was three hours later when Rollison did leave the nursing-home and, in order to keep up the pretence in some ways, he rented his

Gresham Terrace flat as Mr Bernard Brown and the world officially believed in his death.

But he was more worried than he had admitted to Warrender.

He was sure that McNab hadn't talked. He felt convinced that Warrender would never have let the secret out to anyone else than Colliss and Owen. And he was sure of himself and Jolly. That left a short list of suspects, of people who knew of Dragoli, and who might have given the Egyptian information.

He put Anne Farraway at the head of it, although he hated to think she was possible. On the other hand, she had behaved with remarkable self-possession and had blossomed out very differently from what he had first expected of her.

The list was:

Anne Farraway.
Reginald Colliss. (But if so, why attacked?).
Detective Sergeant James Owen.
Dr Alderson, the house-surgeon at
    Grandley's.
Nurse Alice Bligh.

It was no use crossing any of them off, the Toff knew. But what worried him more was the fact that Owen and Colliss were working in the affair and that they might be able to pass on extra information at any time to Dragoli.

Yet nothing happened to worry him in the

141

next week.

Time flew surprisingly quickly. The Toff amassed a large supply of his visiting-cards for he expected to pay many calls when he appeared again. Anne Farraway visited the place once and assured him that she had not breathed a word even to her fiancé.

'Is he still holidaying with you?' asked the Toff.

'Yes—he's in London today.'

'Doesn't he *ever* work?' demanded Rollison plaintively.

'Well—he does more or less as he pleases. He's a representative for a big wholesale chemist and if he gets one or two decent orders he doesn't have to worry about working for a few weeks.' The girl smiled cheerfully. 'I'd like you to meet him.'

The Toff was looking thoughtful but nothing like so thoughtful as he felt. It was a point of considerable interest that Ted Frensham, fiancé of Anne Farraway, should be an employee of a large chemical company. For no way of distributing snow would be better than under the guise, say, of boracic powder or one of a dozen other harmless white powders.

'That's an idea,' he admitted. 'Especially if he isn't overworked. Why are you so anxious about it?'

Anne shrugged her shoulders. She was dressed in a flowered frock and a light swagger coat, for it was a warm day, and she looked cool and delightful.

'Well, he's not a fool, Rolly'—they had progressed considerably, since they had first met, in the method of addressing each other— 'and he guesses there's some reason for me going to stay with perfect strangers. He knows about—well, my earlier adventures; I'd told him about my brother, of course. And he thinks he ought to be able to do something.'

'I quite agree with you,' said the Toff.

Just sixteen days after the explosion at Shadwell he met Ted Frensham for the first time. He hardly knew whether to be suspicious of the man or not but he had to admit that he liked the cut of his jib. Moreover, any idea that he was not worthy of Anne Farraway disappeared.

Frensham was a big man, perhaps shorter than the Toff but considerably broader and thicker. He was fair-haired, fresh-faced and obviously followed outdoor pursuits. When the Toff learned that he was a cricket enthusiast, Anne Farraway wondered whether the men would ever remember that Ted had come on business. But the friendly argument on the merits of the top-spinner against the googly finished, Frensham stretched out his large legs in front of him and threw his head back as he looked at Rollison.

'Now—Anne calls you Browning but—'

Rollison nodded lightly, although again he wondered whether the girl had confided in her fiancé.

'But what?'

'I seem to remember a photograph of the Hon Richard Rollison who died in the course of duty a fortnight ago,' said Frensham with a refreshing grin. 'Correct me if I'm wrong, of course . . .'

The Toff scowled.

'You ought to be,' he said; 'but—look here, Frensham, there's one way you can help me and a contributory way will be to think and talk of me as Bernard Browning. Do you think you can manage that?'

'I do,' said Frensham.

'Right,' said the Toff and he made a fine show of being confidential. At the end of half an hour Ted Frensham had promised to do everything possible to find out whether abnormal supplies of any chemical that looked like cocaine were being distributed anywhere in England and if so, how. The Toff, when the couple went, sat back and wondered whether it would work or whether by some freak of chance he had heard only half of the truth.

Anne's story about her brother had never been corroborated properly. He hated to think she might have lied: but there was a possibility that she was concerned in this affair with a different motive from that which she had professed.

It was true that she had been badly treated by Dragoli; but the Toff was not sure whether that treatment had been inspired by the obvious reason or not. Besides, Dragoli himself might have been deceived . . .

It was on the same evening that Rollison was able to give up the sling, had his arm massaged by Jolly for the last time and planned the next move against the Black Circle.

CHAPTER THIRTEEN

Frensham's Find

Ted Frensham was one of those men, something like the Toff, who have a penchant for impressing others. Frensham's task was to sell chemicals to retailers and wholesalers. He would have been as successful selling silk stockings, knick-knacks or lawn fertilisers. He had a genius for selling and he had succeeded in capitalising it to good effect.

People liked and believed him. If he said a thing was good it was taken for granted and with the backing of Longley, Fare and Company, one of the most reliable manufacturers of drugs and chemicals in the trade, he was able to keep his promises that his supplies were of excellent value.

After leaving the Toff, he had had tea with Anne at a small wayside café on the road to the Surrey home of the Tennants.

'More satisfied'?' she asked him.

Ted scowled with mock ferocity.

'I'm not sure that I approve; he's an attractive blighter. But I wish to heaven you'd told me before just what kind of show you'd been mixed up in. I might—'

'Have tried to interfere and if you knew Dragoli—' She broke off with a laugh that did not ring true and leaned forward with a hand on his arm. 'I daren't risk it, Ted. But with Rollison used to this kind of thing—well, it's different. I wish I'd met him before—before it started.'

'Before they got your brother,' Frensham said slowly. 'Yes, it was a devil, but—'

'It's probably as well for him,' said Anne. She thought little enough of her brother but she hated the way he had died. None the less it was better than if he had been arrested by the police and gone through a trial with the possibility of hanging at the end of it. For she knew that he had committed murder or at least been accessory to one. 'Well, let's try to forget it. You're a fully blown member of the Toff's Army now.'

'Army?' Frensham lifted his brows.

'Pretty well that. He's talked a little at odd times and he has a most amazing crowd of friends in the East End. All kinds of rogues—'

'Thank *you*,' said Frensham weightily.

Anne laughed.

146

'Oh, they're mostly reformed. When he wants to get information he goes to them. He seems to have a soft spot for what he calls the small meat and they—well, they're fond of him. But do you think you can find out what he wants to know?'

Frensham dabbed a warm forehead with a silk handkerchief. It was near the end of August and the past few days had been scorching hot.

'I can,' he assured her. 'There must be a hundred powders that look like cocaine but we'll see. I'll guarantee Longley and Fare aren't in the racket but I'll check up in the warehouses all the same. Worried?'

'A bit,' she admitted. 'I wanted to keep you out of it, Ted. I think I'd break up if anything happened to you.'

Frensham smiled, nodding slowly, reassuringly.

'I know the feeling. But doesn't it occur to you, angel, that I'm just as anxious to stop anything happening to you? Can I have your guarantee that you'll stay with these Tennants until it's all over?'

'Yes.' Her eyes were gleaming. 'I've promised the Toff!'

'I'm asking you, not the Toff,' grinned Ted Frensham. 'Er—not attracted, I hope?'

'I like him and he's a grand chap but—he's not Ted Frensham. I didn't think you could get jealous, darling!'

Frensham looked rueful.

'I'm not used to that kind of competition! He's got a way with him—but away all fears! We'd better be getting on if I'm to be back in time to start the good work in the morning.'

He drove a roomy Talbot sports car, a recent acquisition. Anne was frowning a little as they bowled along towards Godalming. The Tennants lived in the hills behind the town, some hour and a half from London.

The Talbot worried her.

Until a month before, Ted had always driven a Morris that had seen many better days. Because, he had assured her cheerfully, he was saving up to get married. Then he had made one or two extra big sales, taken a good commission, and had blossomed out with the Talbot. It was second-hand, it was true, but must have cost seven or eight hundred pounds.

Was it possible that he had a source of income other than he professed?

She hated the doubt that crept into her mind. It had not really been there until the Toff had talked of the cocaine being sold— possibly-through a pukka chemical firm. And yet it was surely too much of a coincidence to think that both her family *and* her lover were mixed up in the same criminal organisation.

She glanced at him.

He was studying the road ahead, his face set as it always was when he was driving. His lips curved up a little at the corners, the wind was blowing his curly, crisp hair. He had the profile of an Adonis and she told herself she loved him as she had never done before. Just the possibility that anything might develop to make her lose him made her realise that love more than ever.

He glanced down at her suddenly, laughing.

'Have I altered?'

Anne coloured and looked away at the distant fields.

'Only for the better.'

It was absurd. Ted was far too clean to be touched with anything in the way of crime. She was worrying herself needlessly; the fact that she had had nothing to do but moon about the country was giving her a fantastic imagination and she would have to keep it under control.

Bob and Patricia Tennant were in their garden. Tennant sitting in a deck-chair under a spreading oak, Pat weeding one of the flower-beds and wearing a wide-brimmed hat and a flimsy cotton frock. She was taller than Anne, slim, fair and in her way lovely to look on. No one could have called her beautiful although she had one of the most soothing contralto voices, just a trifle husky, that Anne had ever heard.

Her husband was a man as tall as Ted but considerably fatter. A red-faced, jovial-looking man with an unexpected streak of hardness in his make-up when things had to be done. Rollison knew that he and his wife had spent seven out of the past ten years exploring in the Afghan hills, a task that no one who preferred safety to comfort would have attempted. Yet Bob Tennant, lying back there and waving nonchalantly to the newcomers, looked the laziest man in the world.

'Back, then? I wondered whether I ought to trust her to you, Frensham.'

Ted grinned.

'Seeing that you've been looking after her for a fortnight—'

'Not me—Pat,' said Tennant in a deep voice that suggested some alarm. 'I'm no nursemaid, my son, no nursemaid at all.' He frowned. 'Funny thing that Rollison should have asked us to do our duty when he knew you were about.'

His voice grew lower when he spoke of Rollison: he had had a letter about Anne dated before the Toff's supposed death and knew no better than the rest of the world the real truth of the affair.

'He didn't know me,' said Frensham quickly.

'That explains it all,' said Patricia, walking up with a weeding-fork in her gloved right hand. 'Ready for supper?'

'I've got to be off,' said Frensham. 'I'd love to stay, but . . .'

Actually he stayed to supper and left an hour and a half afterwards. He drove back to the factory and offices that night, looked in at his own small office and then went to the hotel

150

in Chelmsford where he stayed when he was not travelling the country.

At ten o'clock next morning he made all the inquiries he could at Longley, Fare and Co.'s warehouses and then started paying calls on various big retailers and wholesalers. No one would have dreamed from his charming smile and his casual questions that he was aiming to get vital information.

But at half-past four—on what he privately considered was the busiest day of his life—he was talking to the buyer of the wholesale distributing firm of Willow and Kellson, of Blackfriars.

Two hours afterwards he was in the Toff's flat, drinking iced beer and wondering whether the Toff, dressed in silver greys and looking more like a tailor's dummy than a man of flesh and blood, was all that Anne believed. *Could* this man have performed those deeds he was supposed to have?

Rollison's eyes gleamed with lazy humour.

'Let it come, old man, I won't bite.'

'Sorry—I was day-dreaming. Well, I think I've got something for you but I can't be sure.'

'Nothing's sure in this wicked world,' murmured the Toff and his interest seemed no keener as he offered cigarettes.

'No-o. Know the firm of Willow and Kellson?'

The Toff reflected.

'Don't they make syrup of figs for gentle

laxatives?'

Frensham grinned.

'They do, as a matter of fact; but they're also taking orders for boracic acid from several manufacturers like ourselves. It's all being bought for re-sale abroad—in one-ounce packets.'

Rollison frowned.

'Small stuff, eh?'

'Incredibly small for export orders.'

'Anyone else doing the same thing?'

'Not as far as I know but I haven't been to many places yet. Of course it may be nothing at all but single-ounce packets would be a nice convenient size for cocaine.'

'My thoughts exactly,' said the Toff. 'Where do they warehouse?'

'Blackfriars. Want me to try and look round?'

'I'd like you to find whether anyone else is concerned in one-ounce packets of boracic acid,' said the Toff. 'We might as well try and find three or four and you can take it for granted that there's more than one firm engaged in the racket. Dragoli may be an Egyptian degenerate but his mind's all there—and he wouldn't put his powder all in one cannon, in a way of speaking. Will you keep at it?'

'Of course.' But Frensham, the Toff thought, seemed a little dissatisfied. He might be wishing to take a more active part in the affair but, on the other hand . . .

The Toff, although he had been in bed or convalescing, had not been idle. He was wondering about the Talbot sports, as Anne Farraway had done.

*   *   *

The Toff called it luck but others might not have agreed. It so happened that the nearest pub to the warehouses of Willow and Kellson was called the River Tavern, two hundred yards from the warehouses, and owned by a gentleman named Winkle.

Winkle was a true name but no one in the world looked the part less. He was a monstrous, over-fed and bloated-looking man, completely bald and, to a casual observer, completely untrustworthy. It would not be true to say that Winkle had not, in his time, broken the law. On one occasion he had spent three years as His Majesty's guest for the trifling sin of smuggling silks and precious stones from the river traffic to the centre of London. But Winkle, who had a honey-sweet voice, was a man of contrast. Twenty years before he had been a magnificent-looking figure of a man and he had married a woman of astonishing beauty—the madness of the war days might have inspired her choice but at least the Winkles had been happy.

He had one child—a girl of eighteen.

153

Winkle had educated her as well as he knew how but he had been handicapped by the death of his wife when Rene had been less than ten years old. From that time Winkle's appearance had degenerated, he had taken to whisky and beer and other things and retained only a doting affection for the girl. When, without his knowledge, she had caught the eye of a certain Spaniard whose morals were untroubled by conscience—the girl had been just sixteen—murder might have been done but for the interference of the Toff.

The Toff had been looking for the Spanish gentleman on a little matter of murder. He had found the gentleman and Rene Winkle in, to put it mildly, an extremely compromising situation.

And he had arrived, with some ten minutes to spare, to spoil the Spaniard's little *amour,* to make Rene Winkle realise what a fool she was and to earn her father's gratitude. Winkle had not said much but the Toff knew that when he wanted service he had only to ask for it.

Therefore he called it lucky that Winkle should be on the spot. But dotted about London, and in most of the vantage spots of the East End, were others whom the Toff had helped in divers ways. It would have been strange had he not had a port of call near at hand.

It was to the River Tavern that Rollison, dressed in a choker, a bright check cap and a

154

suit of reach-me-downs that did not do him credit, repaired on the evening after the talk with Frensham.

Winkle did not recognise him until, when buying a bitter, the Toff let him glimpse one of those little drawings that had seemed unnecessary to Sir Ian Warrender. Winkle's fat, oily face had not altered but he had nodded imperceptibly. A few minutes afterwards he retired to his private parlour and the Toff joined him. They were in conclave for twenty minutes, Winkle nodding or saying yes most of the time—except when he admitted he had never believed Rollison dead—and then the Toff—simply because he was thirsty—went back to the public bar.

He had never had a more opportune thirst.

The bar was crowded with the usual mixture of the maudlin, the drunk, the honest, the criminal, the furtive and the blatant. In one corner was a trio, all unusually furtive. Chokers were well up about their necks and their hats were pulled well down. Winkle made it his business never to ask questions but the Toff did not mind that.

For he had caught a glimpse of the eyes and broken nose of the biggest man of the trio and he was prepared to swear he was looking at Garrotty the Yank.

CHAPTER FOURTEEN

Business Again

It was one of those things that seemed too good to be true. The Toff's eyes were sparkling and there was jubilation within him as he looked away from the man, went to a corner and waited until he had an even better opportunity of studying him. Garrotty—if it were Garrotty—stood slouched in the one corner for several minutes without speaking a word. Then, in a monosyllable, he ordered another drink.

The syllable was enough for the Toff, for it was the simple and over-worked 'rye.' Garrotty was not yet used enough to England to know that if he wanted whisky he had to ask for it and not rye; but Winkle was accustomed to all manner of queer customers and he simply repeated what the man had had before.

In lifting his glass the man showed himself enough for the Toff to be certain. It was Garrotty with two of his men.

The Toff knew, as he left the River Tavern, that he was asking for trouble by waiting and preparing to act himself. If he had been wise he would have been in touch with McNab quickly; Winkle would have sent word and, for the Toff, would have done so willingly.

156

Moreover, Rollison had been off duty for nearly three weeks and was not limbered up. But he had tried his damaged arm out and spent some hours a day for the past few days walking hard. He believed that he was as fit as ever and he was more afraid that Garrotty would scent the police on his trail; while as the Toff—or, to look at, an out-of-work stevedore or wharfinger—Rollison could keep close to the man's heels without arousing suspicion.

He decided to act entirely on his own.

He slouched out of the bar without another word to Winkle. The street was a dirty, dark, and miserable alleyway with wharves and warehouses on one side, a few derelict-looking hovels and houses, the pub and more warehouses on the other. At distant intervals gas-lamps burned a dim yellow glow. It was not an aspect of London at its best but the Toff was glad of the shadows.

He was not alone in slouching near the Tavern.

Three or four men who would have been inside but for the fact that they could not even find the price of half a pint were on the opposite side of the road, staring dejectedly at the pub, two of them with dirty, blackened cigarette-ends hanging loosely from their lips. Farther along the road a man and girl were talking, the man's voice a whisper, the girl's strident and almost menacing. Under the glow of a gas-lamp the Toff could see her painted lips, the mascaraed eyes, her tawdry finery.

She spared a glance for the Toff as he passed but he was looking elsewhere. He did manage to see the man she was talking to. A tall, heavily built fellow with a bowler hat and a muffler. In his way as furtive as Garrotty; and the Toff wondered—but not idly, for there were always things of interest in the incongruities of the East End—why a man of that stamp, and dressed reasonably well, should have been in the middle of an altercation with a street-walker.

And then an odd thing happened.

It started as the Toff had turned at the corner and was walking back. The doors of the Tavern were pushed open. Three men, with Garrotty in the lead, walked out. Garrotty made a bee-line for the bowler-hatted one. The girl drew back, her lips twisted.

There was menace in Garrotty's voice.

'See here, fella, what's de skoit done t'ya?'

'I—I . . .' The man in the bowler hat stammered badly but the Toff was on the *qui vive*. He had no great opinion of Garrotty's sense but he did not think that the gangster would be crazy enough to come out of the pub and deliberately pick a quarrel that would cause him to be eyed with interest by a dozen or more people. Already the loungers were walking across the road—they had no more than a cursory interest, a hope that something would happen to relieve them of the curse of the monotony that made their life.

'You'n me better talk woids,' said Garrotty. 'I'll see ya, sister.'

The man in the bowler hat made no protest. Garrotty took his arm lightly. The other brace followed in the rear and the girl started to walk, flaunting her hips, towards the River Tavern. But in the yellow glare of the street lamp the Toff had seen a smile on the face of the man with the hat. A slight smile, no more than a flash, but enough to confirm to the Toff that this affair was far fishier than anything that could have been taken from the Thames.

There was no hold-up, not even a good pretence of one—Garrotty wanted to see the man in the bowler hat. It was, in its way, a rendezvous, and the girl had played her part in it.

The Toff's mind was humming, not with theories for he saw no sense in trying to imagine what was happening. What was far more important was to find a way of looking after the girl as well as the quartette now disappearing in the gloom.

He decided quickly, taking a chance.

A wizened little man, disappointed of a scene, spat disgustedly into the kerb and half turned. The Toff touched his shoulder and the man spun round with an oath. His face showed all too clearly that a tap on the shoulder meant more to him than a friendly greeting. The Toff hoped to recognise him but failed. He was doubtless one of the host of small-part crooks who lived in daily and nightly fear of the police, perhaps for no greater sin than touting for book-makers.

'Nar then—'

A ten-shilling note was in the Toff's hand, as though he had taken it from the air.

'Find the girl's name and address,' he snapped, 'and give it to Winkle. OK?'

The note changed hands. The wizened man looked staggered but he nodded. Before he could find words, the Toff had swung round and was hurrying along the street. He moved quickly, silently; and it seemed to the wizened man that one moment he had been looking into a pair of agate-hard grey eyes and the next moment there had been nothing to see.

The Toff reached the corner, his heart thumping.

The quartette had not turned towards Queen Victoria Street or Blackfriars. They were moving towards the warehouses lining the river.

And not a hundred yards away were the warehouses of Messrs Willow and Kellson.

The Toff, his eyes gleaming, his right hand in his pocket about the butt of his gun for he was prepared for all things, even a trick, followed them. They turned—Garrotty leading, the bowler-hatted man behind him and the two gangsters following in their turn—down a narrow alley between two towering

160

warehouses. On the opposite side of the river neon signs were glaring and in the reflected red glow the Toff caught a glimpse of the sign on the warehouse wall:

WILLOW AND KELLSON, LTD

The Toff went onwards, very slowly now.

It was almost pitch dark. Only the faint glow of the advertising signs shed any light at all and it was lost as he went farther down the alley. He came—as he had half expected—to a wider road, cobbled, smelling vaguely of horses. The quartette turned left, towards the river . . .

The Toff pulled up short.

Only three of them went on. One stayed behind which was exactly what the Toff had wanted.

He changed his grip from his gun to a black-jack and crept stealthily along the alley. He was giving full marks to Garrotty and the others for they had made no sound on the cobbles or the concrete flooring of the alleys.

Against a distant light he saw the outline of Garrotty's man, slouched at the corner with his hands in his pockets. He was staring along the road, not the alley. The Toff, moving very slowly, very silently, was within a couple of yards of him before he said softly:

'Reach skywards, friend!'

The gangster swung round. The Toff saw

him going for the gun in his shoulder-holster but the other had done just enough. Turning, he was sideways to the Toff and the black-jack came down with a sickening thud on the back of his neck. A single grunt came as the man pitched forward and the Toff stopped him from hitting the ground hard.

He worked fast.

From one pocket he took a roll of wide adhesive tape and sealed the gangster's lips. From another came two loops of sash-cord—the Toff always travelled prepared, having learned the need in the past—all ready with slip-knots and he had his man's ankles and wrists fastened. The whole job took less than sixty seconds and the Toff was breathing hard as he went towards the gates of the warehouse that Ted Frensham had warned him was suspect.

The second of Garrotty's men was outside a small gate in the big, sliding doors of the warehouse. The Toff could see the river between gaps in the wharves opposite and it was much lighter here. Too light for what he wanted but, by keeping to the wall, he was able to remain out of sight but moving all the time.

Five yards away, he saw the man start and turn round. He was peering towards the Toff and, but for the darkness of a shadow from a large pile of packing-cases inside the wharf, he must have seen the interloper. The Toff waited for ten pregnant seconds and then the other breathed more easily and turned about.

The Toff leapt.

He went like greased lightning, without a sound, for he could jump yards from a standing start. The gangster had no idea that there was anything the matter when a pair of lean hands were at his throat and two thumbs pressed into his jugular. Every ounce of strength seemed to go from his body; then the pressure relaxed and, as he breathed wheezily, an automatic shone in front of his eyes.

The Toff had judged his pressure to a nicety. The man was too exhausted by that sudden, frightening pain to put up a fight and the unexpectedness of the attack had been the chief harbinger of its success.

The Toff relieved him of his shoulder-gun and another from his pocket, as well as a knife and a cosh.

'Quite a wholesale merchant,' he murmured and then his voice hardened. It was no more than a whisper but it made the other feel as though his end was very near.

'Where's Garrotty gone?'

A pair of frightened eyes stared out of a twisted, swarthy countenance. The Toff waited a fraction of a second and then raised his gun. The man gasped:

'In—inside. Wid anodder guy. You gotta say "acid".'

'I've got to say "acid," have I?' asked the Toff and he felt a fierce elation.

'Thanks,' he said. 'Now I'm not going to hurt you.'

As he spoke he slipped his gun into his pocket and, almost with the same movement, brought his clenched fist up with a crack against a fleshy jaw-bone. Two sharp punches did all that was necessary. The Toff repeated the cord tricks and plaster on the second gangster and then lugged him, unconscious and trussed far more conscientiously than the average chicken, behind the friendly packing-cases.

As he went towards the doors of the warehouse he was repeating that he had to say 'acid' and the occasion came a few seconds afterwards.

The door, the only one in the warehouse wall, was shut. The Toff took a deep breath and tapped sharply. There was a pause and then a latch opened.

'Who's that?'

It was a reasonably well-educated English voice, as far as the Toff could judge, and his mind was full of questions as he used the watch-word.

Would it work?

Apparently the speaker had no suspicions of a trick and the door opened. In a dim light he could see a lithe, thin-hipped man *in evening dress.*

It was hard to understand why the fact of the evening clothes made the Toff feel as if he

164

had been kicked hard. He certainly wished he was wearing something different from a pair of gaudy reach-me-downs.

That the other was wearing a small mask, much like a fancy-dress ball trifle, was not so surprising and the Toff did not comment on it, even to himself. But he had another shock when the man said plaintively:

'Put your handkerchief up, you bally fool!'

It was the 'bally' that nearly finished the Toff. He snorted, turned it into a cough and then tied his handkerchief over his mouth and chin. The man in the black mask nodded and led the way to a second door. He pressed a button and the door slid open.

The warehouses of Willow and Kellson were up to date and electrically operated. The Toff was sorry. It might be no easy task to get out again but he was determined to go as far as he could. He had allowed the soft-speaking man to go untouched for others might come, expecting to see him here. Garrotty's men were probably only stationed at Garrotty's orders and only the Yank would realise anything was wrong if they failed to materialise.

The Toff went through the electrically controlled door.

He found himself in a long, narrow passage. At one end hung a pair of heavy curtains; he went towards them and, as he drew nearer, he heard a man's voice, measured, a little high-pitched, like that of a man muttering a prayer.

Dragoli's voice?

The Toff thought so, until he pushed aside the curtains. And then he saw a dozen or more people, sitting on chairs and benches in a big store-room. On a dais at one end of the room—on closer inspection the Toff saw it was the platform of a big weighing-machine—was a little man wearing a black mask, speaking very softly and fluently. It was not Dragoli— Dragoli was a foot taller than the speaker.

The Toff heard the words as he peered about him. He was twenty feet from the nearest man, forty from the speaker. The walls of the store-room were bare, the only other door was behind the man on the weighing-machine platform. The Toff, with the light of the devil in his eyes and an automatic in each hand, prepared to take the biggest chance of his life.

The little man chanted:

'Our arrangements are working smoothly. There will be no alterations until the next meeting. New members—'

'There won't be a next meeting,' said the Toff in a cool, easy voice that was pitched on a low key and yet which reached every corner of the big room. 'Put your hands up, gentlemen— high. Especially Garrotty.'

There was a lilting mockery in his voice, a challenge in the words flung out so nonchalantly; but as thirteen pairs of eyes turned towards him, as half of the men moved and the others jumped up, as Garrotty's hand went towards his shoulder, the Toff spoke again and there was all the threat in the world in his voice.

'Move another fraction and you're finished. I'm carrying fourteen bullets and that leaves one to spare. Garrotty—'

And then two guns spoke in quick succession, two flashes of flame—one from the Toff's gun, one from Garrotty the Yank's.

CHAPTER FIFTEEN

More Suspicions

Had the Toff been working at full pressure during the past three weeks he would probably have adopted different methods; most likely he would have tried to get out of the warehouse without raising an alarm and follow the little man who talked like Dragoli. It might have been the wiser course; but the Toff, with what he called three weeks' rest, was at the absolute peak of confidence and had acted almost as quickly as he had thought. He had never worried about odds; the heavier, the better he liked them. A ten-to-one chance gave him an opportunity for pulling off some unexpected and completely unbeatable stroke where, in a two-to-one effort, the very fact that he was the Toff and he had played such games for years, practically levelled them out to evens.

He had a gun in each hand and he had expected the shot from Garrotty.

He fired a fraction of a second before the gangster and Garrotty winced as the bullet hit his wrist. His gun clattered to the dusty floor and, at the same time, the Toff fired again towards a tall, thin man in evening dress who had his right hand at his pocket. A second gun clattered; and then as the smoke drifted upwards and the echoes of the shooting stopped, eleven sound and two wounded men stared at the tall, lean figure in reach-me-downs, a face that, despite its disguise of grease-paint and dirt, carried the devil-may-care spirit of the man and gave them some idea of the strength in him.

No one spoke but from the passage there was a sharp sound of running footsteps. A single set, if the Toff reckoned rightly. He lifted his left hand, still carrying the gun, to his lips, exhorting silence that he did not think he would fail to get. Then the masked man in evening dress, who had used the word 'bally,' burst through the heavy curtains.

The Toff was standing by them, facing the gathering. His right foot shot out and the youthful man pitched over it, hitting his head against the floor-boards with an unpleasant thump. He stayed where he had fallen for several seconds and then the Toff stirred his posterior with a gentle toe.

'Join the boy-friends,' he said.

The man on the floor started to crawl towards them and the Toff, sensing a trick or an attempt at one, used a toe that was no longer gentle. The man jumped to his feet and sped towards the group of men staring towards the Toff.

Had they been ten yards nearer the Toff knew the chances of success would have been negligible. As it was, he was by no means sure that he would manage to bag them all and if he tried he would probably lose the lot. The most comforting thought at the back of his mind was that Garrotty's men would not bar the way out.

One thing was certain: he could not persuade any one of them to go for the police and there was no telephone at hand. He could not lock the door on them for the curtains made that impossible; perhaps it was one of the reasons why they had been installed. If he went out of sight they would move, perhaps towards another exit. But he certainly could not stand where he was for hours on end and hope that something would turn up. For the first time he wished he had asked Winkle to get in touch with the Yard; then he comforted himself with the thought that he might have failed to get anywhere at all had he been timid.

The little man had been speaking as though

169

at the end of his instructions. The arrangements, he had said, were working smoothly and there would be no alterations. Probably in five minutes, ten at the most, the meeting would have broken up. Before the police could have reached the spot the mice would have scurried to their holes.

No, it was better as it was.

The Toff broke the silence mockingly.

'Well, gentlemen, we seem to be stuck. Don't make the mistake of thinking I'm kind-hearted, you with the bowler. You've seen a little of the shooting and I assure you I can do better. Anyone care to say a few words?'

No one did.

'The man on the weighing-machine,' said the Toff, 'can unmask.' The little man obliged, promptly, but still no one spoke.

'Well, well,' said the Toff mournfully, 'you must be shy. It doesn't matter, the police know ways of making you talk; those I want McNab to have, that is.'

There were three distinct oaths; an 'Oh, hell!' and the sound of a very deep breath. There was more disquiet in the eyes of the thirteen men—all except Garrotty and the little masked speaker—than there had been a few minutes before. The Toff smiled engagingly. He had pulled his mask down for no one here would recognise him, although some doubtless guessed he was the Toff. For the moment he did not propose to confirm the truth or otherwise of their guesses.

'Someone sounds worried,' he said. 'All right, let's start the procession. We'll alter the methods and move in single file instead of circles. Listen carefully, my friends, for I'm in a touchy mood. The little man with the sad voice—yes, you,' he added as the speaker jerked his head up, 'will lead the way. Turn round and walk backwards towards me.'

He expected another attempt to fight but nothing happened as the little man obeyed him. At ten paces the Toff stopped him and:

'Bowler Hat, I'll take you next.'

He was particularly interested in Bowler Hat. The man was tall—as tall as himself, Warrender, Frensham. And Bowler Hat obeyed.

'Excellent,' said the Toff cheerfully, 'we're going to get along nicely, I can see. Now the door-keep man join the procession—turn your back and walk towards me. Little man, proceed.'

He was laughing to himself and his teeth were flashing, as the little man came within a yard of him. The Toff almost guessed what was coming for, like an eel, the fellow squirmed round.

Rollison's fist shot out like a battering-ram.

The other was moving towards him and he took the pile-driver on the point. He went up a foot and then slumped down but three others were moving towards him. The Toff saw them and yet he was elating for none of them drew a gun.

He fired once and his bullet took a man in the thigh. It was all the extra warning needed and the conquest of Bowler Hat and the door-keeper was pitifully easy. Garrotty, nursing his wounded hand, was looking murderous but had never been more innocuous. Three men were lying unconscious near the Toff and a fourth was sitting on the floor with a badly shot thigh.

Then the Toff did an odd thing.

He took his cigarette-case from his pocket and in doing so dropped his gun. He bent down in a flash to pick it up again but kicked it further away.

And he had never seen men move like it.

He had deliberately angled to get away from the door. The mention of the police, he believed, would make the men—unarmed as they were—aim for one thing only: getaway.

He had his left hand in his pocket all the time, in case there was a grab for a gun, but his reckoning was right. Garrotty got left behind in the rush for the door and he paid no attention to the Toff. The crowd threatened to block the passage and the Toff fired a couple of shots over their heads in order to hasten them. He need hardly have worried. Thudding of feet along the passage, the walls of the warehouse shaking, the banging of a door. Someone knew how to operate the electrically controlled partition.

And then a deep, loud voice:

'What the hell's *this?*'

It was a question not likely to be answered for some time but the Toff recognised the speaker, knew that *Ted Frensham* was here and he greased along the passage.

The doors were open. Two men were having a stand-up fight in the small courtyard and there was a thin stream of men racing along the alley beyond.

The Toff, his smile still showing but a large question-mark in his mind, approached the fighters. As he came up Frensham put a hefty left fist beneath a heavy jaw and his man went backwards. He fell almost on to the Toff and the Toff finished him off with a clout behind the ear. While Frensham was staring at that unfamiliar figure, the Toff said gently:

'Can't you obey orders, Frensham?'

Frensham stared.

'Good God— *Rollison!*'

'The same,' said the Toff and his voice hardened. 'What are you doing here?'

In the gloom, Frensham's expression was not easy to see.

'I—oh, damn it, I thought I'd have a look round. You didn't seem to take it in about Willow and Kellson—'

'In short, you tried to see what I was thinking,' said the Toff, as though fully satisfied. 'It's a bad habit but I won't say I'm sorry you're here. Know this part well?'

'I know the bridge, of course, and—'

'Then you'll know the nearest telephone box. Call Inspector McNab, will you, and tell him to come here and to come right in. And then, if you're not too tired, slip round to Gresham Terrace and we'll have a war-talk.'

Frensham stared, and then grinned.

'Right-o. I don't come back here?'

'Not unless you want to get hurt,' said the Toff and Frensham had the choice of two ways of taking it. He seemed cheerful as he swung away while the Toff lifted the man whom Frensham had knocked out and went back to the arena. Now it was over he was beginning to understand the strength of the odds against him.

Then the Toff began to move.

The police should be here in twenty minutes and he particularly wanted to talk to the little spokesman without interference from the police. He would have liked to talk with the bowler-hatted man—in fact, with the whole bunch of prisoners—but one in the River Tavern was better than all five at Scotland Yard.

Hurrying, and without the need for silence, the Toff managed to get the little man to Winkle's place in just over five minutes. There were back ways where no one could see that the Toff was carrying his man and Winkle showed his usual placid front when he

174

promised to look after the 'bloke.' The Toff hurried back to Willow and Kellson's warehouse, to be challenged as he reached the doors.

'Who's that?'

'The Colonel,' grinned the Toff, and Frensham stepped out of the shadows. He had obviously taken on himself the task of guard. 'Have you been inside?'

'No, I thought I'd better stay here. I fixed it with the police.'

'Learning about those orders?' asked the Toff. 'Well, we'll try a little foraging expedition; Mac won't be here for another ten minutes.'

Frensham raised no objections. The Toff, although by no means sure that he could rely on the man, took a chance. He was always taking chances and, if occasionally they let him down, they were far more often the inspiring factors of his successes.

They reached the alley corner where he had parked the first of Garrotty's guards. The man was conscious but the sticking-plaster over his lips prevented him from talking. The Toff slipped the noose from his ankles and Frensham urged the fellow along towards the warehouse.

By the packing-cases the Toff stopped again.

'There's another friend here,' he said, and proceeded to lean over the case, lugging the second gangster up, feet first. In the dim light Frensham's face was a study.

'Damn it, you didn't—'

'You'd be surprised what can be done,' said the Toff cheerfully. 'And here are a brace of Garrotty's boys who'll probably be deported although they'd rather live in an English prison for the time being. Ah—reinforcements!'

It was the squealing of brakes, then the heavy clumping of feet, that broke the silence. Supporting a man apiece, Frensham and the Toff waited. Anne's fiancé seemed to be entering into the spirit of the thing and his grin disappeared as McNab came up with Sergeant Owen and three detectives. McNab stopped short, glaring. He did not know Frensham and no man in the world would have recognised the Toff in that get-up, until the Toff spoke.

'Who telephoned?' demanded the Inspector and the Toff jollied him gently.

'A friend of mine, O McNab, after a shindy that would have warmed your heart.'

'Rolleeson!'

'Better and busier than ever,' said the Toff. 'There are several more prisoners inside, Mac, and I can promise you interesting revelations when you get them to the Yard. Come on, now, put a move on.'

McNab, Owen and one detective followed Rollison and Frensham through the warehouse. Garrotty and the masked door-keeper were still there with the man the Toff had shot through the thigh.

But that was all.

Bowler Hat had gone; and the Toff realised first that *Frensham* had had an opportunity of releasing the man.

Had anyone else been near?

CHAPTER SIXTEEN

Willow And Kellson

The Toff was watching Frensham and the man's expression did not change; he did not seem to be looking at Rollison apprehensively, as if he knew Rollison had expected to find an extra man. McNab, of course, had no opportunity of knowing that there was someone missing, and the Toff decided to keep his mouth closed for the time being.

Rollison wished he had recognised Bowler Hat but there was always the possibility that he would be able to get at the fellow through the girl. On the other hand, the man he had paid to find out her address might have collected his half a sovereign and decided that it was easier to drink it than to follow the girl about. It would depend on his honesty of mind— which had nothing to do with his respect for the property of other people.

McNab looked round from the curtains.

Frensham was against the wall; Owen and the other Yard man stared in astonishment. 'Awel,' said McNab; 'hoo'd ye do it, Rolleeson?'

'As a matter of fact,' said the Toff owlishly, 'I felt a bit worried and I told them I was sending for McNab of the Yard. They looked, my Mac, like men preparing for the gallows.'

'Och, they did, did they?' demanded McNab suspiciously. He had known Rollison for many years but had not yet been able to make sure when the man was serious. 'We'll collect them. Who helped you?'

'Oh, Mac!' exclaimed the Toff reproachfully.

It was not until an hour later, when the crooks were lodged in Cannon Street and Sir Ian Warrender was on the way to the Yard from his Enfield home—he had given orders to be called when any development out of the ordinary was reported—that McNab was convinced that the Toff had managed to do it single-handed. In fact, he was openly dubious when the Toff talked of the nine or ten who had escaped. Frensham could support the Toff there and McNab looked as though he was fully prepared to think Frensham was lying too.

'Awel, if ye did, ye did. But, Rolleeson, ye should ha' sent for me; we would ha' had the whole body then.'

Rollison, lighting a cigarette and sitting in McNab's chair while the policeman kept standing, chuckled.

'And they'd have been gone, Mac.'

'Supposin' they had? We could ha' surrounded the warehouse by nights and they'd have come again.'

That was possible, the Toff knew, but there was no reason why he should admit it.

'Think so? Walls have ears and every flatfoot in the cordon would have been located on the second night—if not the first. Strike hard and hot when the chance comes, Mac. Waiting in this game will get you a bullet in the back, not a brace of Garrotty's men in the dock. Well, I'm off.'

'Ye'll stay to see Sir Ian again, mon!'

'Give him my regards and regrets,' said the Toff, who was still looking like a stevedore in his Sunday-best, 'and tell him that I'm suffering from overwork after my recent illness and the doctor ordered bed. So long.'

Horace McNab had long since given up trying to make the Toff do what he should. And McNab was prepared to admit that Rollison had pulled off a coup that would comprise the second big step towards the stopping of the activities of the Black Circle. The first, at the Red Lion, had also been the Toff's doing.

McNab smiled, a little reluctantly.

'Awel, I've nae doot he'll 'phone ye.'

'I'll lift the receiver off,' said the Toff solemnly. 'I need sleep, my Mac, and lots of it.

Coming, young Ted?'

Frensham went. A cab was passing the Yard as they reached Parliament Street and the Toff hailed it, directing the man to his flat. Frensham leaned back in the darkness of the taxi and said slowly:

'Not so much of the 'young Ted', Rollison. I—'

'Not so much of the high horse,' retorted the Toff. 'If you're going to start taking me seriously we'll dissolve partnership. Joking apart, your information was damned useful; I hope the next lot will be as good.'

Frensham scowled as he leaned forward.

'Confound it, man, you don't want any more?'

'I told you earlier on that there are probably half a dozen places of assignation. Dragoli wasn't there tonight but that doesn't mean he wasn't somewhere else. This is a big thing, Frensham, and there are two points I commend to your attention. First, there were about a dozen present tonight. This organisation is a lot stronger than that numerically.'

'I suppose so.' Frensham seemed a little grudging and the Toff believed he was still annoyed. Genuinely?—or because he was playing a part?

'I know so,' said the Toff. 'And there's something else. A child could have got through that place tonight, knowing the password. I was not impressed by the level of the intelligence that made the preparations. It's not up to Dragoli standard and so—'

Frensham stared, everything forgotten but the inference in the Toff's words.

'But—'

'No buts,' said the Toff. 'I think it's quite possible that we've hit a false trail. It was far, far too easy. In fact, I'm prepared to swear that no cocaine will be found at the warehouse and that Willow and Kellson will be very indignant when they hear that their place has been used by the Circle. No, I'm too tired to argue,' he said, smiling a little. 'We'll sleep on it. Using my spare bed, or . . .'

'I've booked at the Regal,' said Frensham.

'Right o—I'll say good night.'

A little later, the Toff reached Gresham Terrace and went upstairs. But despite his protestations of weariness he looked alert and full of life when he reached his flat. He changed quickly and in ten minutes he was dressed in silver greys. No trace of the stevedore remained.

It took him ten minutes more to get ready to leave the flat.

He had reason to believe that he might be watched but, as far as he could see, no one was after him that night. He would not have been surprised to see Frensham but Anne's young man had gone.

The Toff took another cab and presented

181

himself, just before midnight, to Winkle.

The fat man was in the back parlour of the pub. His daughter was preparing a snack and she looked up at Rollison with a wide smile. The Toff, not for the first time, was taken by the elfin beauty of the girl. She was small and slight with a perfect complexion that it did not seem possible to retain in the East End. Her blue eyes were very large and clear.

She had no illusions now about life. But she was grateful to the Toff, even though she held no romantic notions about him.

'Hallo, folk,' said Rollison cheerfully and sat down at Winkle's invitation. 'I'm afraid this isn't a social call. Where's the boy-friend?'

'Upstairs,' said Winkle, who spoke as little as he could and whom a stranger would have called surly in the extreme. 'I had a messich, Mr. Rollison.'

The Toff's eyes widened hopefully.

'You did, eh? From . . . ?'

'The Weasel,' said Winkle. 'A pick-pocket.' He made a habit of speaking out of East End slang when he was with the Toff, a tribute to the fact that the Toff came from the West and therefore should not know the other language. 'Here.'

He handed the Toff a slip of paper, on which was written:

Daisy Lee,
10 Randle Street,
Lambeth.

'The spelling's all right,' said Rollison, 'the Weasel must be educated, Wink.'

'They do say,' said Winkle with an effort, 'he was eddicated at a publick skule, Mr Rollison. You was wanting to see the man upstairs?'

'I was,' affirmed the Toff.

Half an hour afterwards he came down again, dissatisfied and puzzled. The little man, without his mask, proved to have monkeyish features, a yellowish skin and a pair of venomous eyes. But all the Toff's methods of persuasion—and he knew plenty—failed to make the man talk. Methods used against a Londoner, or Garrotty, were useless against the stoicism of the East and the Toff did not waste a great deal of time.

He went back to the flat, still cautiously; no one seemed to be watching him but the Toff did not believe that Dragoli would let him go without being tailed. That suggested there was someone in a flat opposite on guard and the Toff promised himself to investigate the next day.

There was another investigation that he wanted to do before long.

If the police had not already aroused Messrs Willow and Kellson they would be at the offices first thing on the following morning.

Rollison, with the help of a telephone directory, located them by telephoning gentlemen of the same name and with the same initials. And he hardly knew whether to be surprised when he discovered that they were both at Willow's house in St. John's Wood. And, in response to the Toff's urgent pleading, they agreed to see him if he called within half an hour.

Kellson had done the talking and had consulted Willow at every half a dozen words. Rollison had an impression that the man was a little apprehensive but the Toff stuck to his first statement—that his business was of vital importance and could not be conducted over the telephone.

A great deal had happened in a few hours; less than four had passed from the moment when the Toff had left the River Tavern to when he rang at the bell of Willow's house in Dane Street, St John's Wood.

It was one of a number of large, impressive-looking houses, surrounded by nearly an acre of garden—a large area in that part of London. Willow, apparently, had plenty of money; no one without it could have lived in Dane Street and kept his household at the standard it should be; or so thought the Toff.

With his forefinger on the bell, he tried to tell himself that whatever happened he would keep an open mind. It was disconcerting to find that he wanted to make either Kellson or

Willow a villain . . .

He was surprised when the door opened within a second of his finger leaving the bell-push. A butler, dressed in black, peered at him short-sightedly; it was unusual for a butler to wear glasses.

The man was otherwise unremarkable. He was middling-sized, a little bony and with a slightly paunchy stomach. His voice was as dull and expressionless as any the Toff had heard.

'Mr Bernard Browning?'

'Yes,' beamed the Toff, intent on making a good impression.

'Mr Willow is expecting you, sir. Will you please step this way?'

The Toff stepped over the threshold and surrendered his gloves and stick. The lighting was good but subdued. It showed that Mr James Willow was a man of taste with modern tendencies. The furniture was walnut and, here and there, chromium plating glinted its pale silver reflection. The carpet was good but not ostentatious; a mottled brown and fawn.

The butler reached the second door on the right, leading from the front porch, opened it and, in a deeper voice than he had used before, announced Mr Bernard Browning. The Toff kept his right hand very near his pocket.

A short, fat, fussy-looking man in a dinner jacket and with his stiff boiled shirt-front gaping open where a stud had parted company, stepped sharply towards him, his hand outstretched. The Toff shook hands; Mr. Willow's palm, despite its plumpness, was cool and his grip was firm.

'Good evening, sir, good evening. I don't know how I can help you but your telephone message was worrying. Yes, worrying.' He stood peering at the Toff, apparently as short-sighted as his butler, and Rollison just waited, prepared to hear anything. Willow seemed to hope for some help but he went on at last, his voice somewhat high-pitched, his red lips moving in a careful articulation of every word; like a man, thought the Toff, who had taken lessons in elocution and could not forget his first principles.

'It is Kellson I can't understand,' he explained. 'Most concerned, he seemed. And another telephone call came soon after yours. Kellson had to leave at once; he refused to explain but told me he would try to get back before two o'clock. I wish—I wish I knew why, Mr Browning.'

CHAPTER SEVENTEEN

Disappearance Of Mark Kellson

The Toff also wished he knew why.

He did not let his curiosity prevent him from studying Willow. The little fat man seemed far more perturbed than the circumstances warranted and the Toff was prepared to wager that there was something else weighing heavily on his mind. Willow, in fact, looked like a man who badly wanted to talk, as though he had been worried for a long time and had been keeping his anxieties to himself.

Of course, it might be a nicely set trap.

'I'm sorry Mr Kellson's out,' said the Toff cheerfully, as though he was not particularly perturbed. 'He can't have been gone for long?'

'A little—a little over a quarter of an hour.' Willow blinked and then suddenly remembered his duties to a visitor. 'Sit down, please. Please sit down.'

Rollison obliged, not sorry to take the weight off his feet.

'Will you smoke? A little drink?'

The Toff's case was in his hand. Willow shook his head and the Toff selected a cigarette and lit it with deliberate care. He could see the little beads of sweat on the man's forehead and his upper lip.

'Well, well?' The words came out like bullet-shots. 'What can I do for you, sir?'

'Tell me,' said the Toff very gently, 'how long have you been so worried, Mr Willow? And why?'

The words came out slowly. Willow's eyes widened until they looked like little white circles with the small blue pupils darting to and fro. His hand reached for his bow tie and fiddled with it.

'What—what do you mean, sir?'

'Isn't it obvious?' murmured the Toff.

And then Willow did what the Toff had hoped. He started to talk. The words poured out in a stream and there was no pausing to make sure that each one was pronounced carefully. James Willow was revealed as a rather common little man who usually managed at some effort to control his accent.

'Yes, yes, I'm worried as hell! I don't know 'ow you know, but—listen, Browning! I've been too scared for a month to walk about without worryin'! Afraid they'll get me, the swine. They'll get me and Kellson; they'll break us as they've been tryin' for a year. Threats, threats—my Gawd, if they don't stop they'll drive me crazy! Crazy!'

Willow stopped. He was breathing hard and his lips gaped open. The Toff moved quickly to a small sideboard, lifted a decanter and poured a finger of neat whisky into a glass. He

188

did not trouble to add water but handed it to Willow. The man drank it down without a protest and spluttered as the spirit bit at his throat.

'Here—here!' He had recovered something of his poise. 'I don't reckon to drink it neat, sir!'

'It'll do you good,' said the Toff easily. 'Now, who's been threatening you and why?'

Willow glared at him.

'I—I shouldn't 'ave talked. Who—who are you?'

'I'm not a member of the police force,' said the Toff easily, 'and I've certainly no ill intent towards you, Mr Willow. In fact, I could almost say that I'm a friend. I fancy that this "they" of yours are making themselves unpleasant in many ways and I want to meet them. Now you've said something, why not tell me the whole story?'

Willow sat back heavily in a chair. He looked like a little round ball in it but his eyes were frightened again, the momentary indignation gone.

' 'Ow—how do I know you're not connected with the police?'

'You'll have to take my word for it.'

Willow started to bluster but that did not last for long. The Toff, using that persuasiveness of his, worked his man to the right state of mind and then listened to the story of James Willow.

'It' had apparently started a year before when Willow had received a threatening letter, identical with one that Kellson received on the same day. The threat was of disclosure of a habit that Willow and Kellson Ltd had developed of evading customs duty on certain imported raw materials. Willow did not explain how the duty had been evaded but admitted it was done. The total sum over a five-year period had been over forty thousand pounds.

The Toff admitted that they had operated it cleverly.

So far as the partners knew, no one but three men confidentially employed knew of the evasion. Those three men were quite reliable—or Willow believed.

Then the blackmail had started.

The firm had paid out small sums at first, then larger ones. At the same time, and with belated caution, they had stopped evading the duties. But if the truth was revealed they stood a risk of serving a prison sentence and at best paying a colossal fine.

They had kept paying but the demands had grown larger; Kellson—from Willow's talk Kellson was the stronger man of the two and obviously the leading spirit—had determined to refuse.

For three months—the blackmail had been paid monthly, to the Leadenhall Street branch of the National United Bank and to the credit of a Mr Jones—they had made no payments. Then threats of murder had begun . . .

Willow finished. His frightened eyes were fixed appealingly on the Toff and Rollison felt sorry for the fat little fellow.

'So—so you see . . .'

'There are odds and ends I don't see,' admitted the Toff. 'How did the gentlemen start on you?'

'You mean, how did they communicate? By telephone, sir, by telephone.'

'I see. And all orders were given that way?'

'Yes, yes, they were.'

'You have no idea at all of the identity of the blackmailer?'

'No, no!' Willow jumped from his chair and started to pace the room. 'We have nothing at all, Browning, not a clue! What could we do? If we refused, if we tried to find out anything, we would be reported to the police. It would break our business—one of the biggest in England. You understand?'

The Toff did understand.

He did not belabour the unhappy Willow with the obvious; that if Willow and Kellson had kept out of crime they would have had nothing to fear now. The situation had to be faced.

It had nothing to do with cocaine on the surface but there was a way in which the two affairs could be connected. If Willow and Kellson could be easily blackmailed into paying heavy money for silence, could they not as easily be blackmailed into holding cocaine—as boracic acid, for instance—and sending it to various parts of the country when the orders were received?

It was possible but Willow denied any other kind of pressure. He seemed lost and frightened which was not remarkable; and he was scared by Kellson's sudden departure.

The Toff waited until three o'clock but no word came from Kellson and the Toff decided it was unlikely he would return. What message had taken him away?

Should he have gone to Dane Street without consulting Willow by telephone? He had given the other man a chance of a getaway, and yet . . .

Unless Kellson had been told that Browning was Rollison, and dangerous, why should he have gone? And who but members of the Black Circle would have passed that on?

As he slipped between the sheets, The Toff told himself that instead of getting clearer, Frensham's discovery had made the situation messier. He had asked Willow about the one-ounce packets of powder but Willow had told him they were for special export orders and seemed in no way concerned with them. He did not know that they signified anything out of the ordinary—if, indeed, they did—unless he was playing a part and deceiving the Toff: a possibility that Rollison preferred to ignore.

He just did not believe it.

*   *   *

At ten o'clock the next morning, when Jolly stood by his bed with a telephone in one hand and a tea-tray in the other, the Toff stared up owlishly and tried to collect his thoughts. He looked at the tea longingly and at the telephone with distaste.

'Who is it, Jolly?'

'A gentleman, sir, asking for Mr Browning.'

The Toff took the telephone, to hear the agitated voice of James Willow, as he had half expected.

'Hullo—Willow here—Willow. Kellson's not turned up at the office—he wasn't home last night at all. I can't—'

'What's his private address?' asked the Toff quickly.

He heard it, told Willow not to worry, drank his tea and bathed. He was wrapped in a long bath-towel when the telephone rang again: this time it was McNab.

'Ye've been to Willow,' said the Chief Inspector heavily.

'Tell me something new,' implored the Toff. 'Of course I've been to see Willow. You've heard that his partner disappeared?'

'I have—but, Rolleeson, yon Willow doesna' seem to me to be telling the whole truth. But there's no trace of cocaine in the warehouses.

193

He seemed scared, ye ken. What did he tell ye?'

'A lot of things I promised not to tell you,' said the Toff. 'And as it doesn't seem to affect the Black Circle, I don't propose to—yet. Any of the prisoners talked yet, Mac?'

He seemed to ignore the fact that he had just refused information to the police and McNab, who knew him too well to hope to force a statement, said that some of the prisoners had talked but not a great deal.

'Sir Ian would like to see ye,' the Inspector finished. 'Will ye come round?'

'As soon as I can,' promised the Toff.

But as he breakfasted he felt worried. Five or six prisoners and none of them with information worth a damn. Their silence was made more effective by the fact that the warehouses of Willow and Kellson were innocent of snow.

Each prisoner—except Garrotty and his men, who had simply refused to talk at all and seemed to think that the English methods of interrogation were there to be laughed at—said that they had met weekly at the warehouse for the past year. That they were usually given large parcels at the end of the meeting and were told where to take the stuff. Usually it was to private houses and the police had one or two addresses. The houses were always different, the prisoners claimed that they had no idea what was in the parcels and—

194

a point that made even the Toff believe that they were telling the truth—that they were paid five pounds each week for doing their job. Each man, moreover, was on the fringe of that community called the underworld; small-part thieves, pick-pockets, minor forgers. The men who had escaped, it was said, were all of the same category.

The little man had always done the talking and given instructions. Not one member of the party had officially known the other but apparently during the year the mask rule had been more a matter of form than anything else and everyone knew each other. On the previous night there had been one stranger, apart from the Toff.

Rollison almost expected Warrender's words.

'A tall man, Rollison, wearing a bowler hat. He was taller than any of the others present, that's why they picked him out.'

The Toff was saddened because he had let Bowler Hat go but said nothing beyond:

'Well, you've found one method of distribution.'

'That gives us no clue at all to the source of it or the leaders,' complained Warrender. 'I'm beginning to think it's been well established. There might be a hundred similar organisations up and down the country.'

'For once, we're agreed,' the Toff said slowly. 'Of course it's well established. We first learned of it when Farraway was murdered because he had threatened disclosures—all right, all right,' he broke off, as Warrender looked likely to interrupt, 'you heard of it first when Farraway threatened to talk to you and, if you'd agreed to his terms, you might have saved yourselves a lot of trouble *and* Farraway's life.'

The Toff was smiling but there was a hard note in his voice. Warrender looked uncomfortable.

'Farraway might have been lying—we had to try to make sure.'

Rollison shrugged.

'That's true. And it gets us no forrader.'

'What's this about Willow?' asked the AC.

The Toff, sitting on the corner of the table and swinging his right leg, looked at the older man steadily.

'Sir Ian,' he said, 'I'm not talking and I'm making a request. Don't try to force Willow to talk. Get hold of Kellson if you can—there's a call out for him, I take it?'

'There is.' Warrender spoke stiffly and the Toff went on:

If you knew what I've learned about Willow, you'll have to take steps against him. You're a policeman and the police can't shut their eyes to any kind of crime. Willow isn't—as far as I know—a murderer or a coiner or even a bucket-shop specialist. But he's broken the law and—'

Warrender broke in sharply:

'You're withholding information.'

The Toff leaned back, his face set in mock alarm.

'My dear man, I'm always withholding information until the right moment for disclosing it. Or what seems to me the right moment,' he added. 'Let Willow carry on. If I'm right, we'll have a chance of getting at the Black Circle through him—either the Circle or Kellson. At the moment, one is as important as the other. Once let it be known that Willow is suspected by the police on any account and the bait's no use. Are you following?'

Warrender looked dissatisfied.

'If Willow's playing an important part in this affair—'

'If it'll satisfy you,' said Rollison more abruptly than usual, 'I've no information to suggest that he knows anything at all about the Black Circle. I think Dragoli has been using him but Willow hasn't known it. There's a complication that can only be straightened out by watching and waiting. But if you're going to try and bring pressure on Willow—'

Warrender shrugged.

'We'll leave it for the time being.'

'I think you'll be glad,' said Rollison. 'Now, I've a lot to do. You haven't a photograph of Kellson to spare, have you?'

'McNab can give you one,' said Warrender. He stood up, smiling faintly. 'Sorry if I've been

197

short-tempered. It's easy to forget what you've done but—'

'Forget it,' said the Toff but he felt pleased that Warrender was not annoyed. 'It's what I'm going to do that matters.'

'May I have advance information?' asked Warrender, half-jokingly.

The Toff's eyes gleamed.

'It may not seem part of the show, Warrender, but I'm going to pay a call on a lady who is not as good as she should be—I think. I'm going on business so you needn't assume the worst. So long.'

*　　　*　　　*

The Toff had an unpleasant shock before he made his projected visit to Daisy Lee. For McNab and two officers had just come from a search of Kellson's house and there they had come across an unposted letter—or what had seemed to be a letter—to Miss Anne Farraway, c/o Robert Tennant, Esquire.

Actually the envelope had been empty but it had been enough to make McNab think hard and to bring back to the Toff all his vivid but unwonted doubts of Frensham *and* the girl.

Why should the missing Kellson write to Anne? And, more important, how had he learned her temporary address?

CHAPTER EIGHTEEN

Daisy

McNab supplied the photograph of a man who looked thick-set and swarthy, who wore a thick clipped moustache, possessed a heavy chin not unlike Reginald Colliss's and who was apparently devoted to the butterfly type of collar. It was, in fact, that of a man who seemed dressed twenty years behind the times. The features were heavy and the Toff did not think he would have a great deal of trouble in recognising Mr. Mark Kellson from the photograph.

It was one of those dark, miserable days that drop on to England in the middle of summer, as though to offer gloomy promises of the autumn and winter ahead. A slight drizzle was falling, although it was unpleasantly warm and the sun occasionally tried to gleam from watery clouds.

The Toff, driving his Allard, left the Yard at twelve o'clock, crossed Westminster Bridge and made his way through the rabbit-warrens in Lambeth towards Randle Street, at Number 10 of which lived a lady named Daisy Lee.

A brief study of a post-office map of London had helped him to locate the street. It was one of a few in the East End that he did not know well but it would be easy to get at. One of the things about it that puzzled him—although he realised that it was probably sheer coincidence—was the fact that the street was within five minutes' walk of the Steam Packet and Blind Sletter's place.

The Toff had neglected Blind Sletter lately because he felt that the man had given shelter to Garrotty but knew nothing of the Black Circle. He might be wrong, he admitted, and he put it on his list for further investigation; he would not be able to go there as a waiter again.

As he drew up outside 10 Randle Street, Anne and his doubts were forgotten.

It was a short thoroughfare containing some twenty houses, all of them of three storeys. There was a drab air of semi-respectability about the place which the Toff was well prepared to believe would be found unreliable. Most of the houses were probably let in flats or single rooms and others of Daisy Lee's profession probably rented their apartments close by.

The possibility that Daisy was not all she seemed had to be taken into account and the Toff—again—tried to keep an open mind as he rapped on a rusting iron knocker. There was a pause, a shuffling of footsteps and finally the door opened to reveal a dirty, bearded old man staring at him with red-rimmed eyes. The man's clothes were smeared with the gravies and beers of a decade and there were little bits of tobacco and tea-leaves decorating the dirty grey beard.

'Good morning,' said the Toff. 'I'd like to see Miss Lee.'

'Eh?' The ancient cupped a hand behind his ear, pushing that blue-veined and grimy organ forward. The Toff repeated the request and the ancient summoned a watery and beery smile from some distant past.

'Hee, hee! Daisy's in but it's afore the usual time, mister. *Dai-see! DAISEE!'*

His voice, when he raised it, was surprisingly deep. He stood across the doorway, apparently determined that the Toff should not get in if Daisy Lee did not want to see him. There was a pause and the man was about to shout again when a door upstairs opened and a woman's shrill voice came floating downwards.

'What is it, Ben?'

'There's a feller t'see yer!' quavered the ancient.

Send him up!' called Daisy Lee.

She apparently understood none of old Ben's sense of timing. The ancient tittered as he stood aside for Rollison to pass and the musty smell that the Toff had already noticed grew stronger. It lessened as he mounted the stairs.

A door at the end of the first landing was ajar. Rollison reached it and tapped. Daisy Lee called, 'Come in,' and the Toff entered.

201

The room was larger than he had expected and was furnished with bright new furniture which suggested that Daisy was prospering. A large divan, covered with red satin, stood with its head to one wall and there were walnut-veneered dressing tables and a tallboy, a small table loaded with empty breakfast things and the shells of three eggs.

She was sitting in an easy chair, dressed in a flimsy dressing gown. Over the arm of one chair were a pair of stockings and a needle was stuck in one, a line of thread floating from it.

In daylight she looked less ostentatious than she had on the previous night. There was a suggestion of prettiness about her, not yet worn off. Her teeth were good and, despite the rouge and lipstick, she looked almost wholesome. Her hair was ruffled, as though hastily taken out of curlers.

She looked put out when she saw but did not recognise the caller but her smile came back quickly.

' 'Lo, fella. How'd you get my address?'

'You'd like to know,' smiled the Toff and he sat down on the divan as she waved her hand towards it. The door was closed and the room was oddly silent after the noise in the street. 'Daisy, are you and money good friends?'

Obviously, it was not the usual opening gambit.

'What's biting you, Big Boy?'

She was going to be trite all the way and

yet—she might be able to give information. He offered her a cigarette. She leaned forward to take it. 'I'm here on business which is a little out of the ordinary. I want information and you can give it to me.'

Her fingers, with reddened nails that looked barbarous, were holding the case. He saw the smile fade and a vixenish expression cross her face. Before he realised what was coming the case came at him and he had to dodge hastily to avoid it. Daisy was on her feet, her voice quivering and her hands clenched and shaking.

'A nark! Git out of 'ere, you nosy, interfering squirt! Git—'

The Toff, leaning back on the divan, beamed at her.

'Let it rip, Daisy,' he said. 'And then look at this.'

He slipped a card from his pocket and tossed it to her. Perhaps his nonchalance stopped her outburst, perhaps she thought the card was money. At all events she grabbed it and looked down. She saw the little drawing of the top hat, the monocle and the cane and the Toff saw her anger disappear, saw alarm on her painted face. She sat down heavily, wide eyes staring at Rollison.

'The—the Torf!'

The Toff was puzzled by her expression but understanding came as she burst out:

'But you're *dead!*'

There was a moment's silence. The Toff

reflected that he had forgotten that debatable factor. It showed that the 'official' report of his death had been taken seriously by those who had reason to know the Toff and he realised also that it gave him a power he had not previously possessed. A man had risen from the dead . . .

Perhaps the Toff was one of a few who realised the real simplicity of people like Winkle, Rene, Daisy Lee and others.

'I assure you,' he said earnestly, 'that it was an exaggeration. I'm very much alive. I was alive last night when you were talking to a boyfriend outside the River Tavern and if you can give the name and address of the gentleman it's worth a pony.'

He was eyeing her easily; she seemed to find difficulty in breathing at first and then she muttered:

'Gawd, it *is* 'im! Lissen, mister, I ain't—'

'I hope,' said the Toff gently, 'that you're not going to lie. It won't get you far, it might be awkward later and it will lose you twenty-five good English pounds—the easiest money you've earned in your life.'

She clutched a flimsy gown about her.

'Where's the catch?' she demanded and the Toff knew she was back to normal. He laughed, his teeth flashing.

'There isn't one, Daisy. I'm not after you. I'm after the Man in the Bowler Hat. What's the story?'

204

As he spoke he took out his wallet. A small wad of one-pound notes changed hands. Daisy crossed her legs and drew her chair closer. The Toff was as sure as he could be of anything that he was going to hear the truth.

He was as convinced ten minutes afterwards.

She had known Garrotty, it seemed, and visited him at the Steam Packet. Sletter had a short list of ladies for the delectation of his guests. On the previous day Garrotty had visited her flat. He had asked her to be at the River Tavern and to meet the Man with the Bowler Hat. They were to repair to Daisy's flat for an hour and then come out again. Near the Tavern Daisy was to start arguing and when Garrotty came up was to drop out of sight. For her trouble she had been paid five pounds.

The Toff nodded as she got that far.

'I'm following, Daisy. Bowler Hat came here?'

'He did, mister. But—' She glanced down at the twenty-five pounds and clutched them more tightly. 'But he never told me his name. I c'd recognise him, though, he was a tough-looking bozo with a prickly moustache.' She screwed her lips up in a comical *moue* of disgust. 'He—'

But the Toff was taking something from his pocket again. Daisy looked down at a photograph in his hand and jumped up from her chair.

205

'Gawd, they tell the truth about you! That's *'im!'*

The Toff did not move. It was a shock, although he afterwards told himself that he should have been prepared for it. As it was, he was trying to find a reason why Mr. Mark Kellson should have gone to such pains to visit his own warehouse.

For Kellson had been Daisy's guest on the previous night; always assuming, of course, that Daisy was telling the truth.

CHAPTER NINETEEN

Scare!

The Toff, in those days, did not need to worry where his next few pounds were coming from. He promised Daisy Lee another pony if she told him—through Winkle at the River Tavern—if Garrotty or anyone from Garrotty got in touch with her and then he left 10 Randle Street.

He believed she would tell him.

She had been impressed unduly by the fact that he had apparently come from the dead; and she was aware of his reputation. She was probably more afraid of the Toff than of anything else on two feet and again he had good cause to thank his reputation. It rarely occurred to him that he had built it up and he had only to thank himself.

So the Toff reasoned.

Old Ben, with a finger twisted in his beard, was lounging against the open front door. The drizzle had not stopped and there was a greasy wet film over the macadam-topped road. The Toff put half a crown into a gnarled but ready hand and stepped across the pavement towards his car.

It was the shout from above that saved him.

Daisy's voice, raised in alarm, fear, terror.

The Toff glanced up and saw the man outlined against the window on the other side of the road; and saw the gun in his hand.

Flame flared and there was a soft coughing sound. The Toff's knees doubled up and he crouched behind the Allard, snatching at his pocket for his own gun. A second shot and a third came, clanging into the side of the car. The Toff, still out of sight, opened one of the doors and then slid along the front seat. His legs were sticking out of the car on the one side and he could just reach the handle of the far door.

He opened it slowly, all the time desperately afraid that there might be shooting from behind him or from a floor above that on which the gunman was shooting. He could see through the gap at last and he brought his gun into play.

He was not using a silencer and the shooting

seemed to roar up and down Randle Street. Bullets pecked into the window, glass smashed and plaster fell in a shower. A bullet smacked against the side of the car.

The man at the window swung round and was out of sight in a flash.

The Toff hesitated, only for a fraction of a second but enough for him to get the affair in its proper perspective. If he tried to get across the road he might be shot down; if he did not act soon the gunman would get away.

And then he remembered the ruse at the Red Lion.

It had worked once and there was no reason why it should not help him again. He squirmed upright and no shots came. The clutch went in and he raced the engine for a moment before swinging the wheel and driving for the house on the opposite side of the road.

He did not see Daisy Lee standing by her window, nor the bearded ancient on the floor, gasping, with blood coming from his shoulder and his chest. He was concerned with one thing only: getting the gunman.

The Allard roared across the road and bumped against the kerb. The Toff jammed on the brakes and pulled up less than six inches in front of the small wall surrounding the house. The car seemed to be moving when he leapt from it towards the front door.

It was open.

Gun in hand, he went through the passage.

The door of the front room—where the gunman had been standing—was also open and on the floor was a trail of blood. The Toff raced towards the back of the house but the door leading to the kitchen was locked.

It was not a perfect specimen of the doormaker's art and the Toff rushed at it. At the second effort its hinges gave way.

Against one wall a terrified child was crouching. Steam was spouting from a kettle on the gas-stove and a saucepan was boiling over noisily. But the door leading to the small garden was open and over the wall the gunman was climbing.

The Toff fired from his hip. The youngster screeched in terror and the man dropped down. The Toff raced towards the wall but as he went he pitched over a small, broken doll's pram and he went flying.

His head and the concrete surface of the garden—no more than a courtyard with a couple of small flower-beds filled mostly with weeds—connected with a thud. A red mist crossed the Toff's eyes and he felt his senses whirling. He did not lose consciousness completely but could not move for some seconds.

Slowly into his ears came the wailing of the child and the shrill blast of a policeman's whistle. Rollison managed to pull himself up. He sat on the ground for a few moments while he saw the heavy body of a policeman blocking the passage—the garden door was exactly opposite the street door.

The policeman came ponderously through.

He saw the child and Rollison found a smile although his head was aching like the devil and there was a smear of blood over his hand when he wiped it across his brow.

For the policeman stopped to say:

'All right, little'un, you needn't cry. I'll look after you.'

The Toff managed to stand up while the policeman came on. The wailing had stopped; such was the influence of the Metropolitan Police Force. A large, stolid man, with a pale face and very thick lips, stared at him.

'What's all this?'

The Toff drew a deep breath.

'Attempted murder, shooting with intent to harm, driving without due care and attention, you can help yourself.' He took a card from his pocket with his left hand and a whisky flask from his hip pocket with his right. He presented the one as he lifted the other and the policeman's head jerked back. Rollison had presented a clean card, without drawings, but the name Rollison was enough.

'Here, this won't do. Mr Rollison died—'

'Oh, my obituary notices!' exclaimed the Toff. 'If I'd thought of this I'd never have arranged it. Constable, take my word for it, clamp on it and ask Chief Inspector McNab about it on the quiet. I'm Rollison and . . .'

He sketched the story of the shooting. The policeman seemed uncertain but there was a pub on the corner of Randle Street and he telephoned the Yard from there. What he heard from McNab seemed to satisfy him, although he looked at Rollison much as Daisy Lee had done.

Daisy was not one of the crowd that had collected, the Toff saw.

'All right, sir.' The man nodded ponderously and Rollison wondered whether he would be able to keep his discovery from the ears of the five other policemen who had arrived. It was not a matter of vital importance but it would be as well if the announcement of his 'recovery' was made public via the Press rather than by rumours.

'The Inspector asked you to go and see him, sir,' the man added.

'Thanks. I'd like to collect statements first. What's happened to the old man?'

'Ambulance took 'im while we were 'phoning,' said the policeman gloomily. 'Nasty wounds he's got.'

'Poor old boy,' said the Toff slowly. There was one thing he hated above all others; the harm that sometimes befell people not directly concerned in the case. 'I must go and see him. Whose house did our friend shoot from?'

'Couple called Miller,' said the Robert. ''Usband's at the docks, looking fer a job. 'Is wife goes out charring. The kid'—the man broke off, as though he had just stopped himself from saying what he shouldn't—'she looks after the dinner and Miller'll be back soon.'

Rollison felt sick at heart.

The girl was no more than eight or nine; she was older, even at that, than he had first suspected. And she had to look after the midday meal while her out-of-work father was at the docks trying to get employment and her mother was out scrubbing floors.

He was not surprised when the man Miller arrived to tell his story. He was a little man with a straggly moustache and a pair of tired but defiant eyes. Unexpectedly, he spoke without the emphatic Cockney accent of most of the local inhabitants.

'I didn't know who he was,' he reiterated. 'He said he wanted the front room and he paid five shillings a week for it.'

'When did he start?' asked Rollison.

'Ten days ago. Oh, damn!' Miller broke off and the Toff saw tears in the man's eyes. 'We shan't get *that* now . . .'

'Easy goes,' said the Toff. 'And don't worry. You'll have to repeat your story once or twice but you'll be all right.' He slipped a pound note into the man's hand. He would gladly have made it ten but that would have been asking for trouble. Money could go to the head of a man like Miller quicker than strong wine, after a long spell of out-of-work pay. 'Did this fellow look in any of the other rooms?'

'Not—not as far as I know.' Miller was looking at the pound note and then at the Toff. 'I—I didn't like the look of him but five shillings was five shillings. He called himself Smith . . .'

Rollison spent ten minutes at the house and he had an opportunity of seeing that the downstairs flat was spotlessly clean, even if the furniture was second-hand and dilapidated and the oil-cloth badly worn.

He was very thoughtful when he left Randle Street.

Obviously 'Smith' had been told off to watch Daisy Lee. Probably—and it was not stretching the imagination too far—he had taken orders in the past twenty-four hours, perhaps more, to watch for the Toff. It was another angle of the thoroughness of the Black Circle's organisation and it did not make pretty thinking.

The wounded gunman was not picked up. Where he had gone to earth the Toff did not know and tried not to care. A call went out for him, Rollison learned when he looked in at the Yard and told his story.

There was no object in keeping Daisy Lee's information to himself and Warrender promised to sharpen the look-out for Kellson. While the Toff said slowly:

'Have you got anyone watching Willow?'

'Yes. They're not interfering with him—'

213

'All right,' smiled Rollison, 'a bargain's a bargain and I know you'll keep it. But have Willow watched carefully, will you? Two men at a time and armed, if you can manage it.'

'Have you learned something else?'

'Only that it'll pay to be careful,' said the Toff. 'For Dragoli will learn I've been to see Daisy. He'll put two and two together and assume I know that Bowler Hat and Kellson were one and the same. By the way, better have Daisy watched too; they might try to get at her.'

'I'll look after it,' promised the AC.

Rollison, with all the angles blocked as far as he could see, went back to his flat. The more he pondered the position the more he was convinced that if he could find who had given Dragoli the truth about the Toff's 'death' the quicker he could get at the Black Circle organisation in England.

'Anne,' he murmured to himself, 'her boy-friend, Colliss, young Owen—that's about the limit. I—'

He broke off for the telephone shrilled out. As he lifted it he was thinking of Anne Farraway. But he did not think of her for long when he recognised the voice at the other end of the wire.

It was Dragoli's.

CHAPTER TWENTY

Dragoli Threatens

'So you have been lucky again,' said Dragoli.

His voice was chanting, as always, smooth and oddly threatening. Rollison had known no one with the same power of expressing thoughts with the very sound of his voice as Achmed Dragoli.

'It's a habit,' murmured the Toff and he settled himself to talk more comfortably into the telephone. 'You can't say the same, my Eastern friend.'

'Perhaps not,' said Dragoli. 'I shall do soon. Does it appeal to you, Rollison, to know that you have been close to death far, far more often than I have?'

'For an excellent reason,' said the Toff gently and his voice hummed with mockery. 'You *want* to kill me.'

There was a moment's pause before the Egyptian said, more softly than ever:

'Are you trying to suggest you don't want to kill me, Rollison?'

'I wonder?' murmured the Toff and he was in high fettle, playing with words, using that most powerful weapon of his, lumbered as it was with the cumbersome name of psychological terrorism. It was simply a matter of making the other man think that you knew a great deal more than you did and getting him worried. 'You'll be much more use as a witness than a corpse, Dragoli. Did that occur to you?'

'You are talking a lot,' said Dragoli.

'I always do,' said the Toff brightly. 'Let me keep talking, it'll edify you. I've managed to collect a small army of your friends and they're languishing in the unpleasant place called prison. I've busted your Willow and Kellson connection, I've caught Garrotty, I have one of the little ticks you call an organiser . . .'

He paused.

He had staked a lot on that last phrase and he wished he was able to see the Egyptian's face. It was not as important as it might have been for Dragoli's voice gave him away.

'You—you know of them?'

'My dear, beloved Achmed,' drawled the Toff and his eyes were gleaming with a devil-may-care gleam that had something of triumph in it, 'of course I know about them. Organisers up and down the country, all nicely placed for distributing the stuff. I've got one—and he proved more talkative than I expected. Probably more than you did too.'

'Ali—talked!'

'Ali also talked,' lied the Toff cheerfully; he was getting more and more pleased with life every second: now he knew the name of the little man he had collected from the warehouse. 'He admitted being one of a large

216

number, my friend, and that was a help. I'm extremely busy, as a matter of fact, locating some more. You'll be in Queer Street in, as far as I can estimate at the moment, twenty-four hours. That might tempt you to leave the country but I shouldn't try.'

There was silence for a moment and, when Dragoli spoke again, his voice was harsher and expressionless.

'You're too clever, Rollison, but you've made mistakes.'

'Don't get fond of my mistakes, Achmed, I often make them on purpose. What's your next move? Or are you going to try and keep it secret?'

'My next move?' The words came very softly. 'It has been made, Rollison.'

'Do tell me,' urged the Toff.

'I have managed to secure a captive who will be of considerable interest to you.'

The Toff's heart seemed to turn over. An image of Anne Farraway was vivid in his mind's eye. But he kept his voice steady and tinged with mockery.

'Name please, or don't you want to give it?'

'I telephoned you with that specific purpose,' said Dragoli. 'This morning I arranged for the disappearance of that young fool Frensham. He is meddling far too much—like you. Frensham is alive, so far. His girl—I think that is your term—knows it and thinks she knows where he is. At the moment she is

217

hurrying to him, having been warned of the foolishness of getting in touch with you. Are you beginning to understand?'

The Toff had to make a considerable effort to keep his voice steady. 'You've made another of those admirable mistakes, my friend, but perhaps you meant it too. I was prepared to hand you to the police as a witness but if you've hurt the girl again I'll deal with you myself. I'm something,' added the Toff gently, 'of a sadist when I'm roused, especially with Eastern squirts. The word was taken from Daisy Lee but that won't interest you. Listen, Dragoli—'

But Dragoli interrupted, as though he was anxious to finish what he was saying in a hurry.

'Rollison, if you move against me again I'll murder them both. Understand?—both! Keep in your flat for the next day and then arrange to go abroad. Otherwise—'

'Dragoli,' said the Toff very gently, 'you almost convince me, against my will. Almost. Good-bye.'

He rang off and for a moment he was staring at the wall, his face gaunt, the expression in his eyes bleak. And then he moved across the room quickly. He pressed the bell for Jolly and stepped back to the telephone. As he was dialling TOL he spoke to Jolly who had opened the door promptly.

'Get the Yard on the other 'phone, Jolly, and ask them to have a search made for

218

Frensham—you know his full name. Also for Miss Farraway. And hurry!'

Jolly stared; and then the expression in the Toff's eyes made him move. Meanwhile the toll operator was asking the Toff for a number; he called Tennant's house.

There was a continual *burr-burr* but no response.

He fidgeted, cursing, but still no reply came. Twice the girl changed the line, twice she came back with the same answer:

'I'm sorry. There is no reply.'

The Toff hung up.

Jolly appeared in the threshold again, his face unusually animated.

'I—I hope no harm has befallen Miss Farraway, sir.'

'Do you?' asked the Toff and his voice was like a whip. 'So do I. Listen, Jolly. Stay by the telephone and if you get word from Mr Tennant, 'phone me at the Yard right away. And ask him to call the Yard. Understand?'

'I will see to it, sir.'

The Toff's bleak expression changed suddenly and his smile flashed.

'Good man. Dragoli is on the run or he wouldn't have tried this; but I ask you a question, Jolly. Who knew where Miss Farraway was?'

'Well, sir—several people. But she *could* have been followed after she called here, sir.'

'I had a good man on her heels all the time

and he reported nothing,' said the Toff. 'No, my son, whoever let Dragoli on to this also told him that I was still Rollison and Browning was a myth. Good-bye.'

He hurried out of the flat and, although he kept hurrying, he was careful to see that none of the curtains on the opposite side of the road moved. None did. As far as he was able to see, no one was following him and he reached the Yard in ten minutes, after ignoring most of the rules of the road.

Warrender was out: McNab looked up with alarm when his door burst open and the Toff dropped in.

'Rolleeson—'

'Mac, we're narrowing it down. Dragoli knew where Miss Farraway was. That means the leakage was either from the Yard or from Frensham. None of the other suspects knew where she was staying. Get me?'

'But—but you've just asked me to keep a look-out for Frensham,' protested McNab.

'I did—and a good one, for the love of Mike. Frensham might be for or against us— I'll explain the reasoning some other time— and I want him badly. Very badly. Meanwhile, where's Sergeant Owen?'

'Off—off duty,' said McNab. 'Rolleeson, yell not be trying to say—'

'Has Colliss been to the Yard lately?'

'Awel—yes. He was in consultation with Sir Ian only yesterday, Rolleeson. But he—'

'Oh, he's supposed to be reliable! So is Owen and so should Frensham be, perhaps. Did Colliss know where Miss Farraway was staying?'

'He—he micht ha' done,' admitted McNab.

'Then he micht ha' told someone, my Scotsman. Ask him to come up to London pronto, will you?'

'But—'

'Oh, a fig on you and your buts!' roared the Toff and McNab had never seen the man nearer to anger. 'Get him up, man.'

The telephone rang and then McNab looked up after a moment.

'For you,' he said and, as the Toff grabbed the telephone, McNab dabbed his forehead. The sight of energy like the Toff's made him sweat.

The Toff was listening to the deep voice of Bob Tennant; a worried voice too.

'Jolly's just been through,' said Tennant. 'Never mind about your being dead—I can't find Anne.'

The Toff said things that he should not have done, and:

'What happened?'

'Pat and I went for a stroll. Anne was doing some mending and said she wouldn't worry to come. We were out for only twenty minutes and, when we got back, there was no sign of her and she'd taken a hat and coat. I called the exchange and they told me she had had two

221

telephone calls.'

The Toff hesitated and again that bleakness was in his eyes.

'Well, it can't be helped—'

'But damn it!' exclaimed Tennant. 'I—'

'Just stand by and if you happen to see her again, don't let her out of your sight,' said the Toff.

He replaced the receiver and stared down on McNab without smiling. The Inspector looked worried and the Toff suddenly laughed; but there was no humour in the sound.

'I'll be seeing you,' he said.

It was half an hour later when he reached the River Tavern. The pub was closed but Rene opened the side door, smiling widely when she saw who the visitor was; her smile disappeared when she saw the expression on his face.

'Gracious, Mr Rollison—'

'Not now,' said the Toff. 'Is the little boy-friend still upstairs?'

'Yes—yessir.' Rene hesitated and then as the Toff started for the stairs she exclaimed: 'But I must tell you, sir! There's a tar—girl here, asking for you. Name o' Lee. She says she's got an urgent message and she's waitin'.'

CHAPTER TWENTY ONE

Old Haunts

Daisy Lee seemed a little defiant, a great deal scared and considerably more anxious for haste. She looked as though she had dressed in a greater hurry than usual and she spoke quickly, stumbling now and again over her words.

The Toff heard her out.

How she had been to Blind Sletter's place, how, at the Steam Packet, she had seen two more of Garrotty's gangsters and several other men, including a Turk. "E wus a Turk', Daisy reiterated several times, as though she expected the Toff to disbelieve her. And there was also a prisoner, a tall fair-haired cove, whose face had been bleeding something awful.

'How did you know they were prisoners?' demanded the Toff.

The girl's eyes did not drop as he stared into them.

'I know my way about the Packet, see? And the boys are liable to fergit me. I see them, the fella and the girl, in one o' the bedrooms—cross my throat!'

'I'm believing you,' said the, Toff. 'Did you speak to them?'

223

Daisy shook her head.

'What am I—askin' for it? I've took a awful chance, comin' t'see you. I—'

'You took a hell of a chance,' admitted the Toff and his mind was working like lightning, probing into the improbabilities and the possibilities of the situation. 'I'll pay you well for it.'

Daisy looked more reassured.

'You'd better stay here until it's over,' the Toff said.

'What's over?'

'The police raid on the Steam Packet with me as first reserve,' said the Toff and, as he spoke, something seemed to crack inside him. Even Winkle was astonished at his inward fury—a fury that he did not voice but which seemed to emanate from him.

'Blimey!' Daisy gasped, stopped, and then rushed on:

'Mister, I reckon I c'n look arter meself an' I've got a date with my boyfriend. We're going out inter the country, you don't have to worry about me.'

'That's a relief,' said the Toff, without smiling. 'All right, scram.'

Daisy hesitated.

'Got a bit on account, mister?'

Winkle rubbed his fat cheek as though he was prepared for the Toff to do violence. And then the Toff smiled with one side of his mouth.

224

'I get you. In case I don't get out, is that it?'

'A girl's gotta take care of herself,' said Daisy. Her eyes brightened when the Toff took out his wallet. He selected four five-pound notes, rustled them between his fingers and then pushed them towards her. She took them eagerly, grunted 'Ta' and turned from the back parlour. Her high-heeled shoes rapped sharply on the linoleum as she walked along the passage. The side door of the River Tavern opened and slammed to.

The Toff moved as the echoes quivered.

'I'll be seeing you, Winkle, and look after Ali upstairs, he's going to be wanted soon. So long.'

''Ere!' started Winkle but before he could move his ponderous body the Toff had gone in the wake of Daisy Lee.

*　　　*　　　*

A big man, with his mouth and chin muffled up and a bowler hat on his head despite the fact that he was indoors, looked into Achmed Dragoli's amber eyes and shrugged his shoulders impatiently.

'I tell you we've got to get Rollison. The man's more dangerous than the rest put together—'

'I could have told you of that, my dear sir.' Dragoli, still clean-shaven, did not move his eyes. 'We shall get Rollison and we shall do it

225

quickly. In fact, even now—'

He stepped to the window of the house in Camberley and looked out. He had the patience of the devil and the man behind him stirred. Dragoli lifted his hand.

'They're coming,' he said.

In less than three minutes a woman and a man had got out of the car he had seen and a servant opened the doors. Dragoli and the man in the bowler hat waited. The woman who came in was Daisy Lee and she flung her hat on a chair as she half-shouted:

'He bit—he's raidin' the Steam Packet! With the cops!'

'So,' said Dragoli. 'He told you the police would raid the Steam Packet, did he?'

The girl laughed, her voice high-pitched. She looked uglier even than when she had stood in front of the Toff waiting for her money, wondering whether she had succeeded in convincing him or not.

'That's it, I've fixed him.'

If he works true to his past pattern,' murmured Dragoli, 'he will go alone. He will be afraid that we shall get warning of the police and he will try to rescue the girl and Frensham—alone. He is very brave, is Rollison.'

There was a sneer in the Egyptian's voice but the man in the bowler hat looked dissatisfied. He pushed his hat back, revealing his very wide grey eyes.

'Look here, Dragoli, he might have meant it and if the police go to the Steam Packet—'

'They will find Blind Sletter and perhaps some others but no one who can give them any useful information. But I think you are wrong in expecting Rollison to send the police there. The thought of poor young Anne—'

'Not so much of the gab!' snapped Daisy Lee. 'What's the layout if we get the Toff? He's smart.'

'And yet,' murmured Dragoli, 'you were able to deceive him so easily on two occasions.'

The girl laughed mockingly.

'I know his sort, that's why. But if he gets away—'

'It is not likely that he will get away,' said Dragoli. 'If he does we will find another means of ending his career. Don't worry about Rollison. Of far more concern are our own plans.' He looked at the man with the bowler hat, his eyes expressionless. 'You have made arrangements to replace the warehouse at Blackfriars?'

'That's all right,' said Bowler Hat. 'I'll find a place.'

'But have you?'

'Not yet! Kellson's disappearance has made it awkward, Dragoli, but we'll find him. What are *you* laughing at, my sweet?' He drawled the words sarcastically as he looked at a giggling Daisy and the girl stopped laughing.

'Don't mind me, brother. I was laughing at

227

when Rollison showed me that photo and I said you were Kellson.'

The man's lips curved a little in a reluctant smile.

'I see. I won't get annoyed with you, Daisy, because you really have managed very well. To tell Rollison that Frensham was with the girl was a clever touch, I'll admit it.'

'And yet,' said Dragoli slowly, 'we have not yet faced facts, despite these clever touches. Whether we get Rollison tonight or not, we have to admit that he has robbed us of several members. They must be replaced. And the warehouse is no longer usable. That must be replaced! And with Kellson gone we have to find a new method of distributing some of our stuff. On all those points we could do well with more clever touches, my friends.'

Bowler Hat nodded. Daisy Lee sat back in her chair, showing a plentiful streak of silk stockings. There was silence in the room until the clock on the mantelpiece struck eleven.

Bowler Hat looked at his watch.

'That's a minute fast. We'll hear from the Steam Packet any time. I'm scared of Rollison. He would have got me at the warehouse if I hadn't an extra thick skull and managed to get away before the police came.'

Dragoli's eyes were angry.

'Rollison is an unimportant detail in our arrangements. The organisation is all-important and must go on whether Rollison lives or dies. There will always be interruptions, always be trouble, but while we remain free from the police we need have no fears. Remember the money in this and—'

Daisy sneered.

'Listen, Big Boy. You're always talking big about money but we don't see much. I reckon we've handled a hell of a lot've snow for you in the last year and we ain't had more than enough to pay for our keep. Supposing you show more dough and then talk business?'

Dragoli did not speak but his eyes were murderous. Daisy ignored them and went on viciously:

'I've touted the stuff for you an' I've took a lot of the risks. I—'

'You do not seem to understand,' said Dragoli very carefully, 'that in the past week we have been forced to close up several of our outlets. The addresses which the police could get to know from their prisoners, for instance, have been crossed off the list.'

'Sure, they've been crossed off but they're a dozen or so and we feed hundreds. *And* they pay cash on the nail.'

'That's true,' said the Man in the Bowler Hat and he eyed Dragoli curiously. 'You are not playing the fool with the Black Circle, are you, Dragoli? It wouldn't pay you. You may be the kingpin in England but there *are* other countries.'

The Egyptian was breathing very softly.

'I see. There are other countries and you would be prepared to operate in them? Perhaps you are afraid of the police, my friend. Have you forgotten that I first introduced you to the Black Circle? That without me it would never have started properly in England? Are you forgetting that I, and no one else, arranged with Willow and Kellson to handle the stuff for us in the first place and then followed with others? Have you not the intelligence to realise that I stopped using Willow and Kellson as soon as possible, that I have twelve firms in England, each handling the stuff for one month in turn? That I have a foolproof organisation of which you are members? Supposing this had been a Willow and Kellson month? The police would have found the stuff and would have been satisfied they had found how it was distributed. Would they have looked for another eleven firms? Have I not arranged centres in the biggest industrial parts of the country? We three are the only ones who know of that—and Kellson. He is too frightened to talk. He is so frightened that he has disappeared. Well?' His lips were twisted and he looked as though he would gladly have killed the man and the woman. 'What *now?*'

The Man in the Bowler Hat was clenching his fingers nervously but Daisy Lee's hard eyes were fixed on Dragoli's.

'You've fergot something, pal. You've fergot

230

the profits and the shares we ain't seen yet. Talk's cheap but I want my hands on some dough.'

Dragoli took a deep breath.

'You have been well paid. When the arrangements for a distribution of profits come from the Stamboul headquarters you would have been well rewarded. You—'

'Would'a been!' snarled Daisy and she jumped up. But Dragoli had an automatic in his hand and it covered them both.

'You forgot a very important thing, my friends. *I* am the leader in England and my recommendations are carried out. Naturally, I want as much as I can, and now—I am running the Black Circle's business admirably. I don't *need* you. And so . . .'

His gun moved a trifle. Fear was burning in Daisy's eyes; she looked far worse than when she had acted so well with Rollison. And the Man in the Bowler Hat staring wide-eyed at the gun, was trying to speak.

'I shall find it very profitable,' murmured Dragoli. 'This house, of course, is suspect. The police will eventually find it. I would prefer them to find it empty but now they will find two bodies. You see how all my rivals go? Garrotty was useful but he will never shoot again. So were his men. Some have suffered because I could not help them but *everyone* who threatens Dragoli's safety, who might talk if they were paid well enough, goes the same way. Are you understanding now?'

Daisy was on her feet, swaying a little to and fro, her eyes wide open. The man was shivering from head to foot. There was murder in Dragoli's words, in his eyes: death in the automatic. It moved again and there was a grin on the man's sallow face, as though he enjoyed seeing their fear and was reluctant to finish his play.

'You—you yellow swine! You worked for this!'

'I did, Daisy. I have worked very carefully and I can honestly report that the Black Circle will be in danger from you if you live. So—'

Then the interruption came, from the door.

It was a man's voice, harsh and clipped. Dragoli swung round with his gun and fired towards the door on sight. But the man standing there fired first and the bullet took Dragoli's hand—the hand that the Toff had shot badly at the Steam Packet in Lambeth.

Dragoli's gun dropped as Daisy gasped:

'Fren—*Frensham*! How—how did *you* get out?'

Frensham was breathing hard. His coat was torn, his hair blood-stained and there was an ugly wound down his right cheek. But his voice was steady enough.

'Never mind how I managed it. Stay right where you are, Colliss!'

The Man in the Bowler Hat stood still as though rooted to the spot. His heavy mouth

232

and heavy chin were revealed as the muffler dropped away. Colliss, archaeologist and special agent of the police in Stamboul, was gaping at the other man's gun.

Then another voice came.

There was a mocking lilt in it and it seemed to make their blood run cold.

'The answer to my Daisy's prayer, little one; thanks for showing me the way. No, I didn't believe you this time, Dragoli, I found three men and Daisy's chauffeur downstairs and they relieved me of a lot of worry. I offered them money to skedaddle without making a fight and alarming you: and they went. You should pay good wages and you'd get better service. But after hearing Daisy's complaint it's understandable: greed, my Achmed, is the lowest common denominator of the crooked race and if you'd been more open-handed you might have lived instead of getting hanged. With your men gone I freed Frensham and he took the door while I waited by the window.'

The Toff, smiling cheerfully, stepped through the open window from the top of a ladder. Frensham's gun did not move and none of the trio made the slightest move to escape.

They hadn't recovered from their shock yet.

'Rol—Rollison!' gasped Daisy Lee. 'But—but the Steam Packet! You were going—'

'I repeat, I guessed you were lying and I followed you. I'll also repeat that I've heard the whole story and it doesn't show any of you up in a good light. But do tell me one thing: why in the name of Allah did Garrotty attack Colliss if Colliss was working for you? It was the one thing that made me think our archaeologist was honest.'

CHAPTER TWENTY TWO

The Racket

Colliss spoke in a dead voice.

There had been a few seconds of silence, as though the trio were trying to convince themselves that this was true. The Toff, as immaculate and smiling as ever, looked like a ghost to Daisy Lee and Achmed Dragoli. They did not look at Frensham.

'Dragoli—didn't know,' Colliss said. 'Until afterwards. I didn't join until I got to Stamboul—'

The Toff's eyes glinted.

'And they discovered you were a police agent, did they? So they doped you with cocaine until you had to have more and more—and then you joined them. Is that it?'

'That's—it,' admitted Colliss, still in that dead voice.

'Fine!' The Toff's voice was rollicking. 'And thanks to your thick skull you escaped the

234

other night. And what about you, Daisy, while we're learning things? You've been a distributing agent, have you? When Colliss was going to the meeting you had to arrange for him to be taken there so that you could be sure the police weren't giving him watch-dogs. Very nicely arranged. And after you'd led me up the garden you rigged the shooting in Randle Street. Another question, little one—why scream and warn me?'

The woman's eyes were venomous.

'The fool was too slow! There were people in the street and I wanted them to tell the narks I tried to warn you. But you dropped down instead of turning round and he missed you. I wish to Gawd he'd shot your brains out!'

'Now, now,' murmured the Toff. 'And after I've saved you from Dragoli, too. A nice man, our Achmed.'

It was then that Dragoli and Colliss moved.

They seemed to work in unison, although Dragoli started a fraction of a second before the other man. They grabbed the table and uplifted it, hurtling it towards the Toff. Colliss flashed a gun from his pocket and emptied it towards Frensham. The fair-haired man dodged, away from the door and Dragoli and Colliss reached it. Daisy was a foot or two behind them, the Toff was on the floor, making no effort to get up; Frensham was pressing behind a sideboard.

The door was flung open; and then Dragoli

235

saw *the police.* He stood there for a fraction of a second and then swung round. Colliss turned with him, firing towards the Toff, while Dragoli used a second gun, with his left hand, for Frensham. But the Toff was shooting and he found their forearms. He was still among the litter from the table; Frensham was out of the line of fire behind the sideboard.

Dragoli, both arms useless, made a rush for the window but the Toff sprang as though released by a spring. He tripped the Egyptian up and, as Colliss tried to hit him, the Toff's fist crashed under his chin. Colliss went sprawling and when he did get to his feet he was surrounded by policemen.

McNab and Warrender joined the Toff.

The Toff's eyes were still very bright.

'That's a nice parcel for you, Mac, and I can give you the whole racket. It was neatly worked out, I'll admit that. Daisy or Colliss will tell you of the other firms they're using. But—have you had anything from Miss Farraway?'

Warrender looked awkward.

'Not a word, Rollison.'

Frensham swore. He looked a mess but the Toff knew he was prepared to go on until he dropped.

'All right, I'm going to the Steam Packet—'

It was Daisy Lee who spoke, sullenly, on his words.

'You needn't, Rollison. She ain't there. We

never had the little squirt, we only played that on you. We tried to get her with Frensham as a bait but she'd left the place when we went, so we worked on that. Got me?'

*   *   *

The Toff this time was convinced that she was telling the whole truth. With no object for lying, Dragoli and Colliss confirmed it. They had tried to get Anne Farraway but she had left the Tennants' house before they had succeeded.

Two hours afterwards, when the Steam Packet was raided and Blind Sletter, with the two remaining gangsters of Garrotty's brigade, were taken into custody—after a complete rout, for none of them had expected the raid as late as it came: Dragoli had told them it would probably be about ten o'clock—the Toff was forced to the conclusion that the girl had gone off on her own.

'But where?' asked Frensham helplessly. 'She must have had some reason.'

The Toff said nothing.

He was thinking, bitterly, that the only two uncertain things now were the parts played by Anne Farraway and Mark Kellson. No other angle was open. Kellson, it seemed, had been frightened by Dragoli and fled the country.

Had Anne had reason for doing the same?

At three o'clock, with Frensham at his side,

237

he reached the Gresham Terrace flat. Warrender and McNab were at the Yard with the prisoners. Rollison had grown tired of answering questions. How he had believed Daisy up to a point but when she had claimed to have been allowed to see the 'prisoners,' even accidentally, he had found it too much to swallow and realised she was in the racket—a racket, as they had known, to distribute cocaine throughout the country.

Using different distributing centres, like Willow and Kellson's, at different times, Dragoli had reduced the chances of a complete discovery to a minimum. Had he lost one place there were eleven others to fall back on; with Daisy Lee and Colliss dead, Dragoli would have been the only man in England to know everything. Ali—still a prisoner at the River Tavern—had known a little but not enough to do lasting damage to the Black Circle's English organisation.

The one-ounce packets of boracic acid had been a clever stall. Other Black Circle agents ordered them from abroad, so that every so often the cocaine could be substituted without arousing suspicion.

It was all over. Frensham was cleared of suspicion. Owen and the police—except Colliss, who had fallen a victim to snow so easily—were equally clear. Colliss, of course, had passed on the police news to Dragoli.

There remained Anne Farraway.

The Toff seemed to see an image of her gleaming eyes' teasing him a little as he entered the flat. Frensham had not spoken for over an hour. He seemed to the Toff like a dead man.

And then the Toff saw Jolly, fully dressed.

'Good Lord, man, can't you sleep? But as you're up, some strong coffee, and—'

But Jolly for once ignored an order. He closed the door and then opened that of the Toff's bedroom. And on the threshold stood Anne Farraway, smiling a little just as the Toff had imagined.

*   *   *

'Apart from these personal pleasantries,' said the Toff with some irony and feeling very much wider awake, 'what happened, young woman?'

Frensham stood back from Anne, flushing. The Toff was telling himself that there was little likelihood of a broken engagement in that quarter and he was glad. But she was a tantalising little imp!

Anne eyed him thoughtfully.

'Go on,' said the Toff, 'tell me what it's all about. The Tennants are worried to death, the police are searching for you all over the country—and apparently all you did was to walk out of the place and come here. After a telephone-call or so. Who 'phoned and—'

The girl's voice was lower than usual.

'It was—Kellson—who 'phoned.'

'Kellson!' exclaimed Frensham but the Toff waved him back. Anne went on quickly:

'He needed to get out of the country quickly and he wanted to see me before he went. He had a special aeroplane ready, and—he's well away by now. They won't catch him. It wasn't his fault altogether. Apart from—from dodging the customs, and Willow was as much to blame for that as he was, it was—John's fault.'

'John!' Frensham exclaimed and the Toff wagged a finger.

'Don't shout, little man. You mean your brother, Anne?'

'That's right,' said Anne Farraway. 'Oh, it's all been a beastly mix-up, but—Kellson was my step-father. Mother died and for a year or two he—was pretty decent. Then I learned he was fooling with the customs. I left him when he wouldn't stop. But I couldn't get away from the chemical firms, because I met Ted, and—'

'Ted finished you,' said the Toff slowly. 'This doesn't exactly coincide with the first story you told me, sweet one.'

'I know. But this *is* the truth. I wanted to keep Father out of it if I could. He was scared as it was. And John—well, it was John who told Dragoli about the smuggling, put Father in Dragoli's hands. I—I'd always refused to take money from Father. I told you John always sent cash to me and what I did with it. It was true but—I hated their work and the way they made money. I meant to keep clear of it until—I learned about Dragoli and John. Then I saw Father, asked him—and learned he was playing a part. I—I think I would have told the police but'—her eyes gleamed a little, although she looked very tired— 'you came along, Rolly, and you seemed more than capable of looking after things. I warned Father to get away—'

'Well, well!' exclaimed the Toff. 'You 'phoned him ten minutes before I reached him the other day. I'm not so sure you oughtn't to be spanked, but—'

'I couldn't have told you more than you'd found out,' said Anne. 'I'd promised myself to tell you everything, on condition you didn't pass it on to the police, as soon as you were active again. But you move pretty fast!'

'Enough of your blarney,' said the Toff, in mock ill-humour. 'I suppose you two aren't married, by any chance? All right, Jolly'll have to sleep in a chair and I'll have his bed. That'll give you a room apiece and preserve the proprieties. I wonder what McNab would say if he knew it all?'

McNab, to the best of the Toff's knowledge, never knew; nor did Warrender. Kellson was posted in the Yard's missing-but-wanted file and was likely to remain there for ever. If the Toff had any satisfaction out of the Kellson

241

angle, it was the vindication of his belief that Anne Farraway had kept something up her sleeve.

When he sent them a wedding present, two months later, it was with a good heart, even if he wondered a little wryly what he would have done had Anne been free. And James Willow, relieved from blackmail, a bouncing, rather common little man who had not been so light-hearted for years, accepted what appeared to him an excellent suggestion from Rollison: he offered Frensham a partnership and undertook to play no more games with the revenue authorities.

Dragoli, Colliss and Garrotty were hanged when the Frenshams were on the high seas for a month's honeymoon. Daisy Lee was serving ten years in prison, others had long terms to serve. The Black Circle could operate in Stamboul but in England it was broken beyond repair.